RENEGADE RANGE

PHILIP KETCHUM

SAGEBRUSH
Large Print Westerns

First published in the United States by Monarch Books

First Isis Edition
published 2016
by arrangement with
Golden West Literary Agency

A catalogue record for this book is available
from the British Library.

ISBN 978–1–78541–020–8 (pb)

Published by
F. A. Thorpe (Publishing)
Anstey, Leicestershire

Set by Words & Graphics Ltd.
Anstey, Leicestershire
Printed and bound in Great Britain by
T. J. International Ltd., Padstow, Cornwall

RENEGADE RANGE

Linus Coleman is camped in the Black Mountains, par r ng for gold. When two strangers turn up on his ɪ tch and threaten him, demanding his haul at gu int, he shoots them down in self-defence. Wi his dying breath, one of the men tells Linus thɛ am Holloway is out to get him. Travelling to Inc ı Falls to notify the sheriff, Coleman discovers tha Iolloway's malignity has spread further: he has puɪ ased Coleman's father's ranch in suspicious cirɛ ɪstances, and seems to be aiming to take over the hole town . . . But Coleman has no way of prɔ ɪg his suspicions. All he can do is watch and wa hoping for a slip-up — until the day comes wh his gun can become judge and executioner, baɪ ɪg out verdicts against Holloway and his crew.

SPECIAL MESSAGE TO READERS

CHAPTER
ONE

Linus Coleman set up his camp above Indian Falls high in the Black Mountains. For several weeks, then, he worked the west fork of the creek, panning for gold. He found a little — not much, nothing worthwhile. He tried another stream higher in the range but with no better luck. Returning from that trip he found two visitors using his camp. They were strangers, middle-aged, whiskered. The minute they saw him they grabbed their guns, covered him and ordered him to dismount — carefully. Next he was ordered to unbuckle his gun belt and drop it.

Linus did as he had been told but he made a grumbling protest. "This won't get you a thing. What's it all about, anyhow?"

The tall one motioned with his gun. "Where you got it hid — the gold you been diggin'?"

"I haven't found much," Linus said.

"But you got some, even if it's only a handful. Where is it?"

"That what you want — my gold?"

"Jist cut the talkin', Coleman," the tall one said. "Where you got the gold?"

Linus wondered vaguely how the man knew his name, but actually that wasn't very important. More realistically, what was he going to do? In the weeks he had spent prospecting he had accumulated a small pouch of dust — worth maybe two hundred dollars. He could hand it over to these two men, and the loss wouldn't be too great. *But what would happen after that — what was next on the program? That was what he was worried about.*

"Hey, I asked you a question," the tall one said, and his voice had sharpened. "Where's the gold?"

"It's probably in the pack on his saddle," the shorter one said. "Want me to take a look?"

Linus spoke quickly. "I better do that. My horse is a little skittish — ain't used to strangers."

The tall one had stiffened. His eyes had sharpened. "So that's where it is, huh? In your pack?"

His attitude was a definite warning. Linus knew exactly what to expect in the next few seconds. These two men weren't worried about a skittish horse. If the gold was there, they could get it themselves. They didn't need him any more. When he turned away toward his horse he would get a bullet through the back.

He shook his head slowly. "No — the gold isn't there. The gold is buried — I'll show you where. What I got in my pack is a map. It's sort of got to be explained. That is —"

"A map, huh?" the tall one said. "Well, I'll be damned. Let's see it."

"Sure," Linus said. "Just a minute."

2

He was right up against it now. He was making his gamble. He didn't have a map in his saddle pack. He didn't have any gold either. But he had an extra gun there, an old .45 Colt, loaded and in good working condition. If he could get his hand on it, get it out and swing around quickly, he might have a chance. Just a chance. It was two to one — and their guns were still covering him — but he couldn't think about that.

"About this map," he said as he stepped to his horse, and reached for the pack. "It's a little crude, and all the places on it aren't listed. Wouldn't be worth much if I didn't explain it, but it makes a place where I'm going to make a fortune. The gold up there is so thick —"

He was just talking, making sounds. Digging into the pack he found the gun. His hand gripped the butt, and it was cold, and suddenly he was shaky. He took a deep breath, pictured just where the two men had been standing, and then he jerked his hand from the pack, lifted the gun into sight and swung away, turning toward the men. He leaned sideways, too, dropping toward the ground, fired, snapping a shot at the tall one, then another at his companion.

Both men were shouting hoarsely, the short one cursing. And both were blasting shots at him. But the tall man went down, rocking backward, clutching his chest as he fell.

Linus rolled sideways. He whipped a shot at the other man, the short one, who was scrambling away, firing at Linus but not really aiming, heading for cover somewhere. He stumbled and fell, sprawled on his face, then got up. Linus steadied the Colt. He fired again

3

and the short one hit the ground once more. This time he didn't try to get up. He lay where he was, motionless.

The Colt was empty. Linus edged to where he had been standing when he dropped his gun belt. He reached for the holster gun he ordinarily carried, his eyes never leaving the lumpy figures of the two men. The tall one was twitching, moaning. He seemed badly hurt. But the other man still lay motionless — he might be dead or he might be waiting for a good chance at Linus.

With his holster gun ready, Linus got to his knees, then stood up. He looked quickly from one man to the other, then he stepped to where the short one had fallen. A brief examination confirmed that he was dead. From him Linus walked toward the tall one. He was still living, but he had a chest wound. It was doubtful that he would last very long.

Linus took several minutes to relax — to unwind his muscles. He buckled on his gun belt, loaded the Colt and put it in his coat pocket, then walked to where his horse had danced away, off into the trees. He brought the horse back, unsaddled him, tied him, then worked off some of his nervousness building a fire, starting coffee and checking his supplies. He didn't go near the short one, who was dead, but he bandaged the other man, although he knew it was foolish. And he kept his eye on him.

It had been late in the afternoon when he got back to camp, and suddenly now he realized the sun was down and it was growing dark. He started his supper, added more water to the coffee, and made another check of his supplies. A good many food items were gone — an indication that these two men had waited here for several days. What a hell of a thing to do — move into a man's camp, and wait for him to come back, just to kill him for whatever gold he had found. For that was what they had meant to do. He was positive of that. Only by luck was he still living.

In the gathering dusk he looked from one figure to another. He supposed he ought to do something about the dead man — go through his pockets for identification, then bury him. But that could wait for tomorrow. By then, the other man would be dead, too. He straightened, kicked angrily at the fire. Damnit, he didn't like this — burying two bodies — but it was too far to try carrying them to Orotown, the nearest settlement. Of course, when he did get there he would have to make a report to the sheriff, but that didn't worry him. He and Carl McMullen got along fine.

The tall one groaned, then started muttering. He had done this before, his mutterings unintelligible. But this time his sounds made words. Linus moved closer to him and noticed the man's eyes had opened. The man seemed to be looking at him.

He got some water, lifted the man's head and held him. The man tasted the water, but that was all. After he leaned back again he closed his eyes once more. But then he opened them and asked, "How long do I have — I mean — is it bad? Am I checkin' out?"

"That's a bad wound you're carrying," Linus said. "No chance of getting a doctor."

"I reckon — Ned Wilson checked out, too."

"Was he the short man with you?"

"Yes."

"He's — gone," Linus said.

"Didn't have to end — like this," the man said. "Had you — dead to rights. Shoulda finished you. Tell me this, Coleman — you got any color, stashed away?"

"Not much," Linus said.

"Hell with it. I jist wonder —"

"What?"

"I jist wonder — how long you'll last. I don't have to worry 'bout you, Coleman. Sam Holloway'll get you, or maybe Kansas, or maybe Al Durfree. Anyhow you're finished — soon as you get back home — soon as you get —"

His voice grew lower, faded away. His eyes closed. Linus, scowling at him, said, "Holloway — who's Holloway?"

The man's lips worked, but made no sound. A shudder ran over his frame. He groaned and then he might have tried to say something, but the sounds he made didn't form words. In a few more moments he seemed to drop asleep.

Linus walked back to the fire. He tried another cup of coffee, finished cooking his meal and sat down to eat. Now and then he glanced at the wounded man, puzzling about what he had said. The names he had mentioned, Sam Holloway, Kansas, and Al Durfree, didn't mean a thing to him. As far as he could remember, he had never heard of them. And what had the man meant when he had said he would be finished as soon as he got back home? The man's mind must have been wandering.

It had grown dark while Linus was eating. Now he added wood to the fire, to keep it going. Then he hauled the dead man closer to the fire, and covered his body with a blanket. He next stopped at the side of the wounded man, and talked to him. He tried to arouse him, curious what the man might say. But he got no answers. The wounded man wasn't far from death. He probably couldn't have said more.

Linus had a smoke, thinking about what had happened, and what he ought to do. Head back home, probably. Make his report to the sheriff, and clear up his responsibility for the death of the two men. McMullen, he was sure, would accept his story. He had a fairly good record. He wasn't the kind to get in trouble.

The wounded man groaned. Linus stepped toward him, but the man didn't waken, and a moment later he shuddered and his mouth dropped open. Turning away, Linus went back to the fire. He got a blanket, then huddled under it, and after a time he stretched out on his side and tried to sleep.

During the early evening the second man died, and the next morning Linus hollowed out a double grave. Before that, however, he made a double pile of the personal effects which had belonged to the two men. These he would hand over to the sheriff. There wasn't much of value in either pile, but someone somewhere might want the things the men had saved. From some papers he found the two men had been called Louis

Finney and Ned Wilson. And they had come from Texas. El Paso. Or at least they had stopped there.

Linus marked the graves with a cairn. He had a late breakfast, shaved, then struck camp. He found the horses belonging to Finney and Wilson, tied them behind his and started his long trip home. Before noon he was below the falls, and by dusk he was well down toward Rhymer Springs. He camped overnight and rode on early the next morning. From Rhymer Springs he followed the course of the river. He was puzzling, now, over how Finney and Wilson had found him. It wasn't an easy trip to Indian Falls. Not many in Rhymer Valley had been there. Of course, a dozen men had made hunting trips into the Black Mountains, but for good hunting you didn't have to go as far as the falls.

The next night, and still in the mountains, Linus camped early near a wide pool on the river. It was a warm day and the water looked inviting. After he had settled the horses, Linus pulled off his clothes and took a brisk swim. The water was icy, but it sharpened his awareness and put a glow into his body. Stripped, Linus was tall, thin, hard-muscled. He had sloping shoulders, a flat stomach and long, straight legs. His hands wrist high and his face and throat were brown-tanned from the sun and the wind. His hair was black, straight and unmanageable, and he had a high forehead, thin straight nose, lips which could smile easily and a square, stubborn jaw. People said he looked like his father, and was much like him, but Linus wouldn't have agreed. He didn't have the sternness his father had, or his stubbornness, or his iron will. His father, Frank Coleman, had led his own herd into Rhymer Valley years ago, when this had been Indian country. He had been the first settler. He had chosen a place to live and had held it — in spite of Indians, and in spite of raiding outlaws. Things had tamed considerably since then.

Linus dressed, had his supper and sat near the fire scowling. His father, in all probability, would be damned interested in what had happened in the mountains. It might bring a sparkle into his eyes. His father, he was afraid, didn't have too much respect for his youngest son. Linus didn't get roaring drunk. He didn't spill into fights. Homer, his older brother, did. Homer fit the family pattern. But he didn't, and it wasn't the fault of his size. In wrestling, he could handle his brother — he could use his fists, too. And he was just as fast with his gun. Homer said he didn't have the spirit he needed, and maybe he didn't — not Homer's kind.

Linus shook his head, his scowl deepened. This fight in the hills would be slapped against his reputation. Folks would hear about it and would smile knowingly. They would say it was typical of a Coleman. The hell with it. He had been forced into the fight, and if he had come out alive, he had been lucky, and that was all. Just as easily, he could have been killed.

He got up, had a cigarette, and while it was still light, picked a place to sleep. This was his last night in the mountains. By midafternoon he would climb through the cut to the upper valley, called De Sellum's Corner. He could stop there for supper. Jep and Laurie both

would be glad to see him. They were two fine people —
getting old now, up in the sixties, but they had had a
good life.

Linus started early the next morning. He made it to
the cut just after noon, climbed down the rocky trail
to the upper levels of the valley, and stayed close to the
river, slanting southeast. Here at the cut he was at
the valley's narrowest point. Off to his left, and to the
north, a range of the Black Mountains dwindled in a
dozen miles to a hog-back area men called the Malpais
Hills. Beyond the hills was Pueblo Mesa. To the south,
after a few miles, the grass grew thinner. It faded
eventually to a wasteland district, almost a desert. But
the land between, watered by Rhymer River, was rich
cattle country. A man could ride for miles and not find
anything prettier.

Five miles down the river he came in sight of the De
Sellum ranch. It was on land well above the flood stage
level of the river. Back of the buildings was a timbered
area, but here and there, throughout the valley, were
other timbered areas.

Linus didn't see anyone around the ranch as he rode
toward it and when he pulled up at the edge of the
yard, he was frankly puzzled. The corral was empty.
Usually, at almost any ranch, a few extra horses would
be in sight in the corral. Linus pushed back his hat. He
looked from side to side. There was a chicken pen at
the far end of the barn, but it looked empty, too. And
there were no dogs around. Jep De Sellum had several
dogs. The clothesline had nothing on it either.

Instinctively, Linus fingered his gun, making sure it was loose in its holster. He had the strange feeling something was wrong. He peered at the house. The door was closed — the windows, too. And it had been a hot day. But what of that? Maybe Jep and Laurie had gone on a trip somewhere, and if they had they would have closed the house. Probably he was just imagining his fears.

He started to turn away, then changed his mind. At least, he could leave a note. He swung back, rode on to the corral, and dismounted and tied his horse. He didn't have to worry about the other two horses. They were tied to his.

Walking toward the house, he called, "Hey, Jep! Laurie! Anyone home?"

He repeated the call, but wasn't surprised he got no answer. Without much question, the De Sellums were gone. He climbed the porch, tried the door. In common with most other ranch houses, it wasn't locked. Linus opened it and stepped inside.

Laurie had always kept the house spotless, and maybe a week or so ago things had been that clean. Now an accumulation of dust covered everything — an indication that the De Sellums had been gone for some time. And without knowing where they might have gone, Linus felt immediately relieved. This explained the deserted corral, the empty chicken coop and the missing dogs. He smiled at his own fears and turned away, then stopped abruptly, arrested by sounds he heard from outside — a horse pulling into the yard.

Linus stepped quickly to the window. A man had reined up near the barn. He stared at the three horses at the corral. They were grouped together. The man might not have noticed that two were tied by lead ropes, but he must have identified them for he swung toward the house and shouted, "Hey, Lou! Ned! When did you get back?"

"Lou Finney and Ned Wilson," Linus said to himself, and he smiled wryly. "They didn't make it back, but what does that mean, really?"

He studied the man in the yard. He had a young-old face, thin and sharp-featured, and he sat hunched in the saddle. Linus didn't know him, and what had brought him up to this far corner of the valley wasn't easy to guess. But the man had known Finney and Wilson — had known them well enough to recognize their horses, or saddles, and by damn, it might be interesting to talk to him.

"Lou! Ned!" the man shouted. "Come on out. It's Glenn Shattuck."

Linus stepped to the door, moved outside and said, "Hello, Shattuck. Maybe I'll do."

The man, still mounted, leaned forward. His eyes had widened. He shook his head and said, "Who the hell are you, an' where's Lou an' — hey, you're the man they went after — you're the Coleman kid."

"That's right," Linus admitted. "But I don't —"

He broke off what he was saying. Shattuck had clawed at his gun. He whipped it free, but as he fired, his horse danced sideways, and his aim wasn't accurate.

12

"No, Shattuck," Linus shouted. "There's no sense in this. Let's talk about it. If we —"

But it seemed Shattuck didn't want to talk. He was sliding from the saddle, and as he hit the ground he fired again, rolled to the side and half-raised up on one knee.

That gave Linus a perfect target. He used his gun twice, driving one bullet after the other, and he didn't miss. Shattuck jerked higher. The gun he had been ready to use slipped from his hand and he spilled forward on his face. He rolled to one shoulder, seemed to be trying to get up, but didn't manage it.

The dust he had kicked up in the yard still hung in the air as Linus walked toward him, kicked his gun away, then knelt down and rolled the man over on his back. Most of the front of his shirt was soggy with blood. It was easy to guess he had been badly wounded, but still Linus picked the man up and carried him into the house. He lowered him to the bed in the back room, opened his shirt and found some cloth to pack his double wound. Then he went out to get some water. This proved to be a waste of effort. When he got back with the water, Shattuck was dead.

Linus left the man there in the bedroom. He went outside, caught Shattuck's horse and tied him to the corral fence. Back on the porch again, he stared off down valley. Here and there he could mark several clumps of cattle, but at least there were no horsemen in sight, neither on the road nor cutting across country. If the shots here had been heard, he could see no sign of it.

This man Shattuck — who had he been? How had he happened to come here and what had he been in relationship to Lou Finney and Ned Wilson? Linus rolled a smoke, surprised his fingers were as steady as they were. He took a deep taste of the tobacco, then forgot about it, lost again in a puzzle he was unable to explain. He couldn't see the reason for it, but Finney and Wilson had seemed intent on killing him — the gold had been incidental. Then, before he had died, Finney had said that Linus would be taken care of by Sam Holloway, Kansas or Al Durfree *when he got home*. He had thought Finney's mind was wandering when he said that — and he still did — but what had just happened made him uneasy.

The sun was a little lower in the sky. In maybe an hour it would drop below the Black Mountains. Very quickly then it would grow dark. Perhaps that was good. It would be dark long before he could get home, and so before he rode in, he could take a look. But that was foolish. What could have happened at home? His father and Homer were equal to a dozen men.

His eyes darkened. He didn't like what had come into his mind. The toughest man in the country could be brought down by a single bullet. It didn't make any difference how big he was, or how important, one bullet was enough. A gun was a great equalizer. Of course, sometimes it was important who was behind the gun, but the general observation remained true.

He stood looking bleakly down the valley. He wanted to get home in a hurry, but he was afraid of what he might find.

CHAPTER
TWO

The Talbots had an early supper. It was a rather good meal, but no one at the table had much to say. Susan and Jean had been quarreling before they sat down to eat. They continued their feud in the way they glared at each other. Mrs. Talbot divided her attention between the two girls and her husband. She seemed equally concerned over the girls and Weller Talbot. He scowled at his plate, ate very little and was unusually silent.

Talbot was fifty years old. Up to a month ago he hadn't been aware of his age. If he had been asked then how he felt, he would have laughed and made some humorous answer. If he had been asked tonight he wouldn't have laughed. Suddenly and frighteningly, his age and his fears about himself and his family had become major factors in his life. Right now, if he could do what he wanted, he would run, and carry his family with him. But that wasn't an easy thing to do.

He looked up, glanced at Ruth, thin and tired, the strain of her worries showing in her face. He glanced at the two girls. Susan was twenty-two, tall, slender and too beautiful. Jean was eighteen, a hundred pounds of tomboy, maybe attractive, too. He hadn't thought about that. Anyhow, the two girls were distinctly different:

Susan serious, responsible, secretive — Jean reckless, unpredictable, explosive.

The touch of a smile pulled at his lips. He, Weller Talbot, had been a mighty lucky man. He had a fine wife, and the two daughters she had given him were more than exceptional. He had some good land. This ranch he owned, on Pueblo Mesa, was as good as the meadowland in the valley. He had a little money. He wasn't in debt. In fact, life had been pretty good to him — up to a month ago.

His scowl was back. He lowered his head, stared at his plate and thought about what he had to say. He knew there wasn't any easy way to put it, so he dropped it just as it came. "I met Sam Holloway on my way back from town. He said he might ride over tonight."

Someone at the table sucked in a sharp, hissing breath. That had been Jean. There hadn't been a sound from Susan. He took a quick glance at her. Her cheeks were pink and she had lowered her eyes. Otherwise, she sat motionless.

At the other end of the table, Ruth spoke mildly. "After all, Mr. Holloway is a neighbor. If he wants to stop by —"

Jean's interruption was harsh. "If he wants to stop by, we can't stop him. If we tried it, we might get murdered in our sleep."

Talbot was suddenly angry. "Don't talk that way, Jean. Rumors are ugly — unfair. As nearly as any of us know, Frank Coleman sold his ranch to Sam Holloway, open and clear."

16

"Not open and clear if no one else saw the sale," Jean snapped. "And what happened to the De Sellums? Someone tell me. Where are they?"

"They could have left the valley, too," Talbot answered, and his voice hardened. "Stop making accusations until you can prove them. That's a law you should follow — all your life. And at least, by God, as long as you're here, you will."

"I can think what I want," Jean flared.

"All right, think — but don't speak. And if you don't approve of Sam Holloway, keep in your room tonight."

"I'll be glad to," Jean snapped.

She backed down — reluctantly. She hadn't said too much, but still she left him upset. He knew she wasn't satisfied. He wished, suddenly, she were younger, so he could strap her, but even a strapping never had seemed to have much effect. Susan had been much easier to control, and was gentler — much more like her mother.

He glanced at her now, and said, "If Sam Holloway bothers you —"

"He's just been — nice," Susan said. "He knows about Linus and me, too. I don't think Linus went away with his folks. I think he'll be back, any day now."

"I hope you're right," Talbot said gruffly. "And I wish we could stop all this talk I've been hearing."

He got up, looked briefly at Ruth, at Susan, and then centered his attention on Jean. Ruth would say nothing, except to support him. That had always been her way. If she differed with him she would tell him mildly, when the girls weren't around. And Susan would say nothing. She would blow with the wind, gracefully, prettily and with a smile. Jean was the only one who might give him trouble.

He looked at her sternly, and said, "Jean, it is never a mistake to be a lady. Just remember that."

"The women in Katie's Parlor House act like ladies," Jean murmured.

Talbot's mouth dropped open. He didn't know what to say next. Where had Jean heard that name, Parlor House? How could she have known of Katie's? Even in the saloons in Orotown they didn't speak of the place aloud.

Jean stood up, a strange smile on her face. She enjoyed her moment of triumph, then said, "Sorry, father. I'll get busy with the dishes."

Talbot swung around and went outside. It was growing dark but there was enough light in the sky to sift down to the earth and show him the surrounding buildings, the barn, the extra cabin, the sheds, the covered well, the mound of the root cellar, the corral fence and the outhouse. The chicken yard was beyond the barn. A dog came out of the shadow of the porch and moved to join him, but without hurrying. The dog reached up his nose to nudge his leg.

"Hello, Bruce," Talbot said. "At least, you don't give a damn, do you?"

The dog was old, crippled by age, partially blind. Once he had chased after Talbot's horse on every trip he made, went everywhere with him. But he no longer could make it. When Talbot drove the wagon, he usually took Bruce along — but one of these days, now, the dog wouldn't even be able to make that.

18

Bruce could amble around the yard, however, and as Talbot wandered about through the gathering darkness, the dog paced him, dropping to the ground to lie when Talbot stopped.

"Weller!" Ruth called from the porch. "Weller, you all right?"

"Of course I'm all right," he answered gruffly, turning back toward the house.

Ruth met him in the yard, then spoke again, lowering her voice. "You're worried about something. It's Sam Holloway."

"We just don't know him very well," Talbot said.

"You think he's interested in Susan?"

"Well, he isn't married," Talbot said. "He's older than Susan, but not too much, I guess. Sam might be forty. He might even be younger. He's well off or he wouldn't have been able to buy the Coleman ranch."

"He's a well-set-up man," Ruth said slowly. "He has pleasant manners. He's kind of courtly. I think he probably comes of a good family — and I want a good husband for Susan. I don't say it should be Sam Holloway, but I'm not sure it should be Linus Coleman either. She thought she was in love with Linus."

"Linus probably will follow his folks," Talbot said. "He may have done that already. He was off in the Blacks a month ago when his father sold out. I suppose Homer could have gone after him."

"They did sell awfully quick, didn't they?"

"Sometimes things work out that way."

"About Mr. Holloway. What should I do about him? I mean, what if Mr. Holloway wants to take Susan riding? Isn't that sort of rushing it? I mean, shouldn't we know him better before we let him take our daughter out?"

Talbot was scowling again. "Folks don't do the way they used to."

"But the old ways were nicer. When we were courting, you came to see me a dozen times before I went out with you."

"Sam's older," Talbot said.

He pictured in his mind Sam riding out somewhere with Susan. Sam, who had been around plenty — he was sure of that. And as courtly as he might have seemed to Ruth, when he got Susan out alone, Sam wouldn't be the kind to lose much time. To hell with him, anyhow. Susan was too young, too fresh, too sweet for a man like Sam Holloway.

"I think I hear someone coming," Ruth said, and she raised her head and looked toward the road.

"Yes, it does sound as though someone was coming," Talbot nodded. "You better get inside and see if things are in order."

She hurried away, and waiting in the yard Weller Talbot measured his courage, but found it at a low ebb. It would be nice to tell Sam Holloway to ride on, but Sam wouldn't agree. He would laugh and ignore the order. Sam had a way of laughing which was hard to handle. Talbot had to keep something else in mind, too. Some of the men who had come to the valley with Sam looked like hard cases — gun-slingers. Maybe Frank Coleman and his older son, Homer, had been roisterous, noisy when they drank, and maybe they had been too ready for a brawl, but at least there had been a spark of fun in what they did. The men with Sam Holloway were grim-looking, ugly and not at all pleasant.

The noises he had heard grew louder. More than one rider was coming this way. Maybe it wasn't Sam Holloway. Hope swelled in his chest, then faded. One of the two men riding in was Sam, big and bulky, tall and wide-shouldered. He had a heavy voice and his mannerisms were definite. He reined up, swung to the ground and said, "Evening, Weller. Wonderful night. Brought a friend with me. Bern Jorgensen. Good man."

"Hello, Sam," Talbot said. "Glad to meet you, Jorgensen."

"I kinda like company," Holloway said. "Anyhow, as I remembered it, you got two daughters."

"Jean's rather young," Talbot said quickly.

"Not too young," Sam said. "I noticed her in town. She's old enough. Frisky, too."

"I still think she's too young," Talbot said. "Besides —"

"You let Bern handle her," Sam said, and he laughed. "Bern's an expert at things like this. Wish I was younger. I'd like to take the frisky one myself. Tie the horses. Then we'll go in."

Talbot took the reins of the horses. He led the animals to the corral fence, tied them, and in his chest there was a sense of panic. It was bad enough to let Sam Holloway come here to see Susan, but Jean was just a child. And this new man — someone he didn't even know. And not a good man, not if he was any good at judging men. What was it Sam had said about Jean — that she was frisky? And that if he was younger, he'd like to try her? My God, what kind of man was he to barter his daughters, for that was what he was doing.

"Hurry it up," Sam called. "Hurry it up, Weller."

Talbot finished tying the horses. He turned toward the porch, stumbling, hating himself. He wanted to yell at Sam and Bern Jorgensen to get out of here — but he knew he wouldn't.

Jean finished the dishes, then walked to the bedroom she shared with Susan. The latter had sprawled on the bed, her head turned away. She didn't look around as Jean came in.

"You'd better get dressed," Jean said. "What are you going to put on — for your latest beau?"

"He isn't my beau, and you know it," Susan snapped. "I'm being nice to him, that's all. And why shouldn't I?"

"Just don't let him give you a baby," Jean said.

Susan twisted around and sat up. She had paled. "I ought to slap you for that."

"Why?" Jean asked. "What do you think Sam Holloway's after? He's no infant, you know."

"And from what you said to father, you're no child either. Where did you learn about Katie's?"

Jean smiled, and waved her arm. "Just around. You might be amazed how much I know."

Susan's eyes had narrowed. "I think I'll start watching you. You know, the other day in town I saw you and Ken McMullen —"

"He's a good friend." Jean said, and she raised her head, listening. "Horses outside. I guess lover-boy is here."

"He's not lover-boy," Susan said. "I'm waiting for Linus to come back. How do you like that? You wanted Linus yourself, didn't you?"

"You're dreaming," Jean smiled.

There was a knock on the door, then their mother looked in and said, "I believe that'll be Mr. Holloway. Susan — you're not yet dressed!"

"That'll take only a few minutes," Susan said.

She took off the dress she had been wearing, chose another, put it on, then stepped to the mirror and started working on her hair. She had long, sandy-colored hair, slightly curly. Jean's hair was coarser, darker. And Susan had a fairer complexion. She should have had freckles, too, but things hadn't worked out that way. Jean had caught all the freckles.

While Susan worked on her hair, Jean took the bed, and stretched out full length. She heard voices in the main room, men's voices, but she didn't try to listen. She closed her eyes momentarily, thinking about Linus Coleman. She had the horrible feeling she would never see him again. And that hurt. Of course, it would hurt if he came home and fell into Susan's arms — which might happen. But when it came right down to it, Susan probably wouldn't marry him. Linus had a stubborn streak about working his own way, which Susan thought silly. Actually, what Susan wanted was someone like Sam Holloway — with money and position.

Someone knocked on the door, and this time it was her father. He looked in, glancing at Susan.

23

"I'm almost ready," Susan said.

Talbot cleared his throat. He turned to Jean on the bed. "Sam's not alone. He brought a friend — Bern Jorgensen. I think — Jean — it might be nice if you met him."

"Me!" Jean gasped, and sat up. "You mean Sam Holloway brought someone here — to shove down my throat?"

Her father looked down. "I think we should be neighborly."

"No!" The word was explosive.

"But, Jean —"

"No."

"If I ask you —"

She got slowly to her feet, and she was shaking. She was angry, all the way through. In a vague sense she realized her father was in a difficult position, but he had always been too nice. People were always walking on him, and he didn't seem to mind. But she did. She wouldn't take it.

She stepped forward, passed him in the doorway, marched into the parlor and looked boldly at Sam Holloway and the other man — what was his name, Bern Jorgensen? — tall and thin, narrow-faced, thick-lipped, and wearing a smirk. That was it — a smirk.

Behind her, her father said, "Sam, this is my younger daughter, Jean."

"Howdy, Jean," Sam said. "I brought a friend with me, Bern Jorgensen. I think you'll like him."

"But I won't," Jean said.

24

She clipped out the words. She wanted to scream them. She wanted to hit something. Off to the side, her mother was watching. She looked frightened.

Sam threw back his head and roared with laughter. He had a puffy face, wide-spaced eyes, too deep and too small, too sharp and hard. His teeth had slightly yellowed. He said, "Bern, it's like I said — you'll have to manage her."

"I'll manage her," Bern said. "In a nice way, of course."

"Sure. Always be a gentleman," Sam said. "I find it's worthwhile."

"Maybe we ought to take a walk," Bern said, and his smirk was wider.

Jean took another look at the man. It hit her that if he touched her she would scream. Something in his look, in his deep breathing, in his bony hands and in the sum of his person was wholly repulsive, unclean.

"All right," she said. "We'll take a walk."

But she didn't mean that. She meant, actually, that taking a walk was the quickest way to get away. It was dark outside. She knew the yard and the area around it, and she could run like a deer.

Her father raised his voice. "Jean, you don't have to —"

"I'll be all right, father," Jean said.

She turned abruptly to the door, stepped out on the porch, and instantly the hulking Bern Jorgensen followed her, caught up with her and took her arm. Back in the house, Sam said something pleasant, or at least he said something and then laughed. Jean heard him vaguely. She moved toward the steps, and she didn't try to pull away.

"We're gonna get along all right," Bern said, and he squeezed her arm.

Jean didn't say a word but she was breathing heavily, quickly, and her body tingled all over.

"I like to get things on the right trail," Bern said. "Ain't nothin' like a good kiss to set off the evening."

He stopped half a dozen steps into the yard, and swung her toward him — and Jean exploded. She kicked out with one foot and then the other, aiming at his shins. One clenched fist aimed at his face. She used it again and again. For a moment, Bern Jorgensen seemed too startled to put up any defense. He let go of her arm and backed away, uttering a surprised cry.

Then he shouted at her, and he seemed angry. "Damnit, woman. What you tryin'? When I get my hands on you —"

Jean saw him lunging forward. She stepped sideways, whirled away and started running. She circled the corner of the barn and fled into the darkness. Her heart was pounding too fast to be counted, and suddenly she was out of wind. Something tripped her and she fell, and heard footsteps behind her. Bern Jorgensen. He grabbed her, and he wasn't gentle. His fingers dug into her arms. He pulled her to her feet, dragging her close to his body. One of his hands slid down over her shoulders, under her blouse, and he closed his fingers tightly on one of her breasts. His laugh sounded crazy. He shouted, "Hey, look what I found. Bet there's another."

26

Jean struggled to get free. She jabbed with her elbows. She twisted away, fighting grimly, silently. Briefly, she had the impression that someone else was with them, another figure looming up behind Jorgensen. She saw him, then lost him, and then abruptly the man with whom she was struggling seemed to dive at the ground, pulling her with him. But he didn't try to hold her after they had fallen. She rolled away easily. She sat up, started to get to her feet, but was startled by a voice saying, "Easy, girl — easy. Nothing to rush about now."

Off in the shadows, a step or two away, someone was standing — the man she had thought she had seen behind Bern's back. But where had he come from? And who was he? A flash of intuition told her. Only one person in the entire valley ever called her "girl." Linus Coleman! Of course, it was impossible he was here. He was up in the Black Mountains — or he had followed his father out of the valley — or he was dead.

She spoke hesitantly. "Linus —"

He came and stood above her. Tall, thin, a wry half-smile on his lips. She couldn't see the smile but she could imagine it. He said, "Sure, girl. That's the name — Linus. But what's been going on? Who's the man over there on the ground?"

"His name's Bern Jorgensen," Jean said. "I never saw him before, but they practically shoved him down my throat. I think he works for Sam Holloway. Anyhow, Sam Holloway brought him."

Linus helped her to her feet, and stood with his arm around her, but it was merely a supporting arm.

Nothing personal in it. He said, "Holloway, huh? What's he doing here?"

Jean bit her lip. She could have answered that question in several ways. The one she chose she thought was fair. "Susan's a pretty woman, and he's not married."

"Saw a woman with him last night over at our ranch."

"That must have been his sister. Young, dark-haired, very pale skin? They call her Glory. But you, Linus? How did you happen to be here?"

"Came over to see you," Linus said. "But you had company. Noticed that, and for some crazy reason I've turned cautious. The world seems to have been turned upside down. This valley's not the place I knew. What's happened to my father, to Homer, to the men who worked there, to Sarah Ingersol who looked after the house?"

Jean took a deep breath. "You don't know?"

"'Fraid I don't."

Jean started to answer, but before she could she heard Bern Jorgensen groan. She glanced to where he was lying. He was still unconscious but he was stirring — maybe on the point of waking up.

"I'll tell you what," Linus was saying. "I've been wanting to talk to someone, and you'll do fine. Suppose we walk down to the springhouse. Left my horse there, anyhow."

"What about — him?" Jean asked, pointing to the figure on the ground.

"I haven't forgotten him," Linus said. "Look the other way."

His voice had changed. It had tightened. Jean looked at him quickly. She couldn't see his expression clearly, but in the pale starlight his lips were pressed thin and there was a bulge at the corners of his jaw. He was suddenly breathing faster. She could sense his cold anger. She spoke quickly. "What are you going to do?"

"This could be a good world," Linus said. "But not if we have to put up with men like him. I ought to finish him now. Instead — I said look the other way."

He walked to where the man was lying.

Jean shook her head. "I don't think you ought to —"

"Look the other way, girl!"

She bit her lips, looked away and tried not to hear the heavy blows which followed — a boot ripping into a man's body. Then those sounds ended and Linus joined her and took her arm.

She spoke under her breath. "You didn't —"

"No, I didn't kill him," Linus said. "But he won't ride for a time. He won't bother anyone for a long time."

They started for the springhouse and as they walked Jean tried to forget about Bern Jorgensen. In a way she could justify what had happened to him. But how would Sam Holloway take it when he found out? How would it affect her father? And just as importantly, how about Linus Coleman? What was he doing here? And what had happened to him? The Linus Coleman she had known never would have stood above a man's body, kicking him. The Linus she had known had been a quiet, gentle man who never got upset about anything.

CHAPTER
THREE

Pueblo Mesa was a tableland north and slightly higher than the meadows of Rhymer Valley. West of the mesa were the rugged Malpais Hills, and circling above them was a fingering range of the Black Mountains. This range curled down to shut off the eastern edge of the mesa.

At two points on the mesa were old Indian ruins, the sites of earlier civilizations. Occasionally, people made trips there, and someday the ruins might be extensively studied by those interested in such things. People from hereabouts went to the ruins as picnic points, or a man might take his girl there just for the drive.

There were three ranches on the mesa, this one of Weller Talbot's and two farther east. The grass was fairly good, and in the lower areas, here and there, were timberlands. No streams crossed the mesa, but wells could be sunken very easily, and Talbot had several on his land. He had two nearby — one in the yard, for ranch house needs, another about a quarter of a mile below the barn, in a clump of trees. Above the walled well and under the trees, Talbot had built a covering shelter. This springhouse was primarily a place to preserve foods against the summer's heat. It was a nice place, too, for a man to go to escape the heat. And a year ago, Linus had discovered another use for the area. It was a nice place to take Susan away from the others.

He thought of that as he walked that way with Jean, and he wished, half-angrily, that Susan were here instead of her sister. Jean was a nice kid, of course. In two or three years, after she grew up, and if she calmed down, she'd really attract attention. But Susan was already there, girl and woman both. He couldn't blame Sam Holloway for noticing her.

"Here we are," Linus said as they reached the trees and moved into the deeper shadows. "Used to be a fallen log close to the house wall."

"It's still there," Jean said. "Straight ahead."

"My horse is tied on the other side," Linus said. "Just thought it might not be wise to ride in. Glad I didn't."

"You've been up in the mountains?"

"Yes. Above Indian Falls. That's high in the Blacks. I got back to the valley the afternoon before this."

"You didn't go straight home?"

"No. I stopped at the De Sellums, but they weren't home. Then I ran into some trouble. I had had some other trouble in the mountains. So I got cautious. I waited until dark, then went home. It wasn't home any more. Didn't see anyone I knew. Strangers had moved in. I crept in and out."

They had found the fallen log and sat down. Jean asked, "What did you do after you — crept out?"

"Too late to go anywhere so I camped near the river, did a little thinking. This morning I worked down valley but kept out of sight. This afternoon I cut for the mesa. Got here just after your guests arrived."

"Not my guests," Jean said.

He reached for her hand, squeezed it, then let it go. "Sure, girl. Now tell me what's happened."

"There is an official story. Then there are rumors —"

"Start with the official story."

"About a month ago Sam Holloway and several friends came to Orotown. Sam said he was looking for a new ranch, that he liked the Rhymer Valley. He rode here and there, stopped finally at your father's place and, right on the spot, bought it."

"Just like that?"

"That's what they say."

"Where did Father go?"

"They say he headed for Montana. There's some government land there, about to be opened to entry."

"That's not until fall."

"Something else happened. According to Erb Wylie, your father got word his brother had been shot in a range quarrel in northern Wyoming. So your father rushed that way, fast as he could. Homer and Mike Bellows were to pick you up in the Black Mountains. Most people expected you to go with them."

"So it was like that," Linus said slowly. "Practically overnight, Father sold the ranch. At the same time he heard his brother had been injured, and he headed for Wyoming. From there he was going on to Montana, to buy a new range. Homer and Mike Bellows were going to pick me up in the Blacks. Erb Wylie, I guess, decided to stay here."

32

Jean nodded.

"Now what are the rumors?"

She bit her lips. "I can't prove them. But Ken McMullen says it's funny your father didn't find any time to say good-bye to anyone. I know if your father's brother had been hurt, maybe it was important to rush away, but still —"

"Did Erb say that my brother and Mike Bellows were going into the Blacks to find me?"

"Yes. That's what he told the sheriff."

"When did they leave?"

"Three weeks ago."

Linus spoke slowly. "Homer and Mike didn't find me. They could have because Homer knew where I would camp. Instead, two other men showed up. They tried to kill me. I think they worked for Sam Holloway."

Jean caught her breath. "Then you mean —"

"I don't want to say it — don't want to believe it. To begin with, I can't think Father would sell the ranch. But he's gone — and Homer, too."

"What will you do?"

"I don't know — yet."

"That man who worked for your father, and who's still here — Erb Wylie. He might know the truth."

"Yes, he might — or he might not. I know Erb pretty well. He's a weak sister. Lazy, deceitful — you can't believe a thing he says. We wouldn't have kept him if help hadn't been hard to find. And as the work slackened, father was going to let him go. He should have been fired about a month ago — about the time

Holloway arrived — and that's rather interesting. I'll try to reach Erb, but I don't count on much."

"You should talk to the sheriff, too."

"Carl McMullen? Yes, I'll see him when I go to town. I've half lost track of the days. Isn't tomorrow Saturday?"

"Yes."

"Then tomorrow Sam Holloway ought to go to town, and a few of his men ought to be there, too. That'll be a good time to meet them."

She raised her voice. "But, Linus — you can't."

"Why not?"

"They'll kill you."

"No, I don't think they will, girl. I think I'll be perfectly safe — in town. Of course, two of Holloway's men tried to get me in the mountains, but no one else was around. And I bumped into another of his men at De Sellum's, but again there were no witnesses. In town, and in front of others, I've a notion Sam Holloway will have to be friendly. I'll drive in tomorrow and see."

She took a deep breath. "You're just going to — ride into town?"

"That's it — I'll just ride into town."

"Won't Mr. Holloway know what happened to the two men he sent into the mountains?"

"Sure. He probably knows already. I brought their horses back and set them free. They've probably been picked up. And there's a good chance they found the man I shot at De Sellum's. Sam Holloway probably won't be surprised when I show up. He knows I'm somewhere around."

She was silent again, briefly, then said, "Linus, I'm afraid — afraid of what might happen tomorrow."

"Then keep your fingers crossed," Linus grinned.

"I wish I could help."

"You can. You can see Susan. Tell her I'm still alive. Ask her to come to town tomorrow. I'll see her then."

"Yes, I can do that," Jean said.

Her voice sounded strange. Linus looked at her, but then shrugged, remembering that Jean and Susan had the same kinds of conflicts as he and Homer. Minor jealousies intrinsic to a family relationship — and unimportant.

He stood up. "Time to ride on, girl. When you get home, tell them where to pick up Holloway's friend. If I were you I'd say someone jumped him in the darkness. You can say it was me — or you can let it go."

"I'll let it go," Jean said. "You're going to have enough trouble anyhow."

He laughed softly. "Good girl. I'll be seeing you. Want me to walk you back to the house?"

She shook her head. "I can get home alone. What I want to see, first, is you riding away, all in one piece."

"I intend to stay in one piece," Linus said, and he leaned toward her and added, "This is kind of a thanks, and it ought to be all right anyhow, since you're Susan's sister."

He dropped his head to kiss her and he meant it to be nothing but a salute, a friendly gesture. Only what happened was different. Jean's head turned up toward

35

him and her lips, warm and moist and open, caught him and held him for a moment. She swayed closer, up against his body, and through his coat he felt the mounds of her breasts and it hit him that this wasn't a little girl kissing him. Damnit, she had all the potentialities of a woman.

He broke away, gulped and stared at her. It was too dark to see her face, to read her expression, but he could hear her breathing too heavily. And he didn't know what to say.

He mumbled, "Jean — I don't know —"

"I'll be in town tomorrow, too," she said, and suddenly she seemed very calm and assured. "Now you'd better ride, Linus."

"Yes, I'd better go," Linus said.

He did, mounting his horse and cutting down the mesa, but his departure was in the nature of a flight — which was rather silly. After a few miles he reined down, had a smoke and thought about that kiss. Damnit, without any question, that had been a kiss. A grown-up, adult kiss. Not kid stuff. But maybe he should have expected it. After all, time wasn't standing still. Jean was eighteen or nineteen. At that age many girls were married.

"I'll just remember that," Linus said. "And I'll be a little careful about Jean girl."

He rode on, slanting toward the valley and toward Orotown, well down the river. It was a several-hour trip, and it would be after midnight before he got there. Most folks, by then, would be in bed. But why worry about that? It would be enough, tonight, to see Carl

McMullen, who as sheriff shouldn't object to a late visitor. That was part of his business.

When he reached the town, Linus took a brief look at the main street. It looked deserted, everything shut up, no lights in any of the buildings. Back of the street, however, in some of the houses here and there, lamps were still burning. One was McMullen's. Linus reined up in front, tied his horse, climbed the porch and knocked.

"You! Linus!" McMullen gasped when he opened the door.

"Sure. I'll bet you thought I was dead."

"I was afraid you were," McMullen said. "But I'm sure glad I was wrong — and maybe I been wrong about a lot of things. Your folks —"

"No, I don't know a thing about my folks," Linus said. "So don't change your mind completely. You going to invite me in?"

"Sure — sure, come in," McMullen said. "Man, it's good to see you."

Carl McMullen was in his early fifties, a short, heavy-set man, wide-shouldered. His arms looked powerful and that appearance was no illusion. In his two hands McMullen could twist a horseshoe out of shape. He was bald except for a fringe of gray hair, and his puffy face was wrinkled. Maybe he should have been an aging man — and of course he was — but he still could hold his own with nearly anyone in the valley.

Ken, his son, who was about nineteen, was patterned along the same lines as his father, short, stocky and well muscled. The surprise of the family was Mrs.

37

McMullen, thin, little and seemingly old. But that appearance was deceiving. Following the pattern of the family, Mrs. McMullen was wiry, and a tireless worker. In the house or helping the sick, she never stopped.

She was up tonight when Linus came in. And Ken, who apparently had just gone to bed, got up and joined them. Mrs. McMullen greeted him as though he had never been away, but Ken gasped in amazement. He mumbled, "But — but you're dead!"

"Not yet," Linus said.

"I'll warm the coffee," Mrs. McMullen said. "And I'm sure we have some pie. Sit at the table, Linus."

He had pulled off his hat and now he set it aside and walked toward the table, saying, "Thanks, Mrs. McMullen. I haven't had anything like pie for weeks."

"You didn't stop at your place?" McMullen asked.

"I looked through the window — late at night."

"Where have your folks moved?"

He shook his head. "I have no idea."

"How come you came home so careful?"

"Three men were responsible for that," Linus said. "Their names were Lou Finney and Ned Wilson — who came to me in the mountains — and a fellow named Shattuck, who jumped me at the De Sellum place. I think they all worked for a man named Sam Holloway — and all are dead."

McMullen whistled, and across the table young Ken stared at him wide-eyed.

"Want to tell me about it?" McMullen said.

"It was like this . . ." Linus said, and he reported what had happened above Indian Falls, then later in the yard at the De Sellums. As he finished, Mrs. McMullen brought him a cup of coffee and a thick wedge of apple pie. He dug into the pie, murmuring his thanks.

"I've met Shattuck," McMullen said. "He worked for Sam Holloway, no mistake. The other two, Finney and Wilson, I didn't know. But from what you've said, they must have worked for him, too. You say you brought back their horses?"

"Yes, and two bundles of their personal effects. I meant to hand them over to you, but after what happened at De Sellums, I tied the stuff on the horses and cut the horses free. And Shattuck's — although I left his body in the bedroom of the ranch."

"How long ago was that?"

"Two afternoons ago."

"Then by this time Holloway should have found Shattuck's horse. And maybe the other two horses. He could have backtracked to De Sellum's. Must have found Shattuck's body — but he didn't say anything to me. He should have said something. After all, I'm supposed to represent the law."

Linus finished the pie. He took another sip of coffee and then smiled toward Mrs. McMullen. He said, "That was wonderful."

"It was the last piece of pie," Mrs. McMullen said regretfully, "I'm afraid. Would you like something else? I could make a sandwich."

He shook his head. "Don't spoil the taste of the pie. I've had plenty, really."

"Linus, what do you think?" McMullen asked.

"I don't like what I'm thinking," Linus said, and his eyes had darkened. "I don't think my father would have sold his ranch for any kind of money. Or if he did, or was forced to, he wouldn't have left the valley and forgotten about me. Sometimes I didn't measure up to what Father wanted, but I was still his son, and underneath everything we were damned fond of each other."

"So if they didn't sell — and leave the valley — where are they?"

"They're dead," Linus said quietly.

Ken leaned across the table, his face showing excitement. "That's what I said, Dad. Remember. I said they were dead."

"Hey, Ken. Easy," McMullen broke in. "That's dangerous talk. We ain't got a bit of proof — anywhere."

"Then get it," Ken said.

"That's why I came here," Linus said. "To talk about what we could do. Mind if I ask a few questions?"

"Nope — and don't mind if I pace the room," McMullen said. "Think better when I'm on my feet."

"Then tell me how Sam Holloway happened to come to Orotown, and Rhymer Valley?"

"He just came," McMullen said. "Don't know why he came in particular. Said he was looking for ranch property and had heard this was a nice part of the country. Believe he said he came from Texas, but I didn't have no call to question. Didn't look like an outlaw. Seemed to have money. Behaved himself properly. I mean, he went to church, didn't gamble, didn't get drunk, was friendly everywhere. That went on about a week. He had rented horses and he and the two men with him went out riding. Visited folks. Told me after a few days that he hoped someone in the valley would sell him a ranch, but he didn't seem to be pushing it. Didn't make no definite offers."

"How much money did he have?"

"Don't know. He didn't put any in the bank. None at all. Must have kept it in his pocket."

"If he had any," Linus said bluntly.

"Must have had some," McMullen said. "While he was in town he spent quite a bit, here and there."

"What happened, step by step?"

"Didn't see it that way. About a week after Holloway got here he and his men rode up valley, stayed all night at your father's place, I reckon. Anyhow, Holloway rode in the next day, said he'd worked out a deal with your father. He rode back. I was flabbergasted, waited three or four days to see your father or Homer. They didn't show up in town so I rode out there. Seems they'd just left."

"Weren't you suspicious?"

"Sure, but Erb Wylie was there. He said your father got word his brother had been hurt and he was rushing that way. Homer and Mike Bellows had headed for the Black Mountains, to pick you up. Then the plan was that your father, Homer, you and Mike Bellows would settle in Montana."

McMullen motioned half angrily. "What else could I do? I knew your father had a brother in northern Wyoming, that new land in Montana was going to be opened to entry. If Frank Coleman made a good chunk of money on his ranch here, why not try something else? And Sam Holloway makes quite an impression. He's friendly, has a booming laugh. Folks like him. If he's crooked it sure doesn't show."

Linus looked away. "What about the De Sellums?"

"They sold out to Holloway, about a week after your father did. They pulled out by wagon. In fact, they had two wagons. Holloway lent them a couple of men to drive the extra wagon."

"Two wagons — why? They didn't take any of their furniture."

McMullen shifted uneasily. "Didn't know that. Haven't been in the house."

Linus was silent for a moment, then he shrugged. "Holloway must be as clever as you say. He was out to see Susan tonight and if he impressed her, then that's something."

No one made any comment.

"He brought another man with him — Bern Jorgensen. They came outside and Jorgensen got fresh. I happened to run into him in the darkness."

McMullen stopped his pacing, raised his head. "What happened?"

"I did what Jean's father should have done. Jorgensen isn't dead, but I'll bet he wishes he was. Jean's just a kid."

"You're sure piling up trouble for yourself."

"Can't help it, Sheriff. You know what I'm going to do. I'm going to wait until Holloway gets here, then I'm going to show up on the street and wander around.

I'm going to act amazed that my folks are gone. Maybe I'll start someone thinking."

"What'll you do when you meet Holloway?"

"Be as pleasant as he is."

"Most likely you'll get killed."

"No. If Holloway is as clever as you say, he won't jump me right away. But he might set up something — a quarrel with one of his men."

McMullen nodded. He moved back to the table, sat down and said, "Mom, let's have some more coffee. Time we did a little planning."

CHAPTER
FOUR

Mrs. McMullen made a bed for Linus on the couch in the parlor, and Ken went outside and stabled his horse in the barn. Until dawn, then, Linus slept. But he didn't sleep too well. He was excited about the next day. It could be terribly important, but he had no idea what would happen. He didn't think Sam Holloway would start anything himself, but his men were another matter. According to McMullen, the men who had accompanied Sam Holloway and those who joined him later were a hard-bitten crew. Three McMullen was sure were gunslingers. More might be.

The weather didn't look good in the morning. From the window Linus looked out at the low scudding clouds sweeping down from the Black Mountains. Even inside he could hear the howling wind. McMullen went to the barn to care for the horses. He made a judgment after he got back. "Won't rain today, don't think. But it'll stay nasty. Might get some rain tonight or tomorrow. Need it anyhow."

"It's still Saturday," Linus said. "Number of folks ought to come to town."

"Holloway, sure. Makes it here perty often. His men, too," McMullen said. And then he looked at his son. "I reckon you know what you're supposed to do this morning."

"You mean, I'm not to talk," Ken said, grinning.

"Don't even think," McMullen said. "Like we planned last night, we want to stage things right. And you keep out of it. Stick to your job."

"What is your job?" Linus asked.

"I'm working at the feed store. I thought you knew it."

"Didn't remember," Linus said.

"He's saving his money," Mrs. McMullen said. "He's going to Santa Fe this fall. He's going to study to be a lawyer under Judge Bellweather."

"Why, that's wonderful," Linus said. "Ken, I had no idea you wanted to be a lawyer."

"Better than running a store," Ken. "Or chasing cows. Might take a couple years to get anywhere studying law. Might even take longer, but I think it's worth it."

McMullen cleared his throat, "You get in front of a bullet and you'll never make it to Santa Fe. Just remember that."

"I'll look after myself," Ken said, and he didn't sound worried.

They had breakfast and a little after that McMullen and Ken left the house. Then, left with Mrs. McMullen, Linus insisted on helping with the dishes. Following that, he shaved, then squinted at his reflection in the mirror. His hair needed trimming. Once, up in the mountains, he had hacked it down with his razor edge, but he hadn't done a very good job. In the mountains he hadn't been concerned too much about how he looked. But very probably he would be seeing Susan sometime during the day, and if he could go to the barber —

"Mrs. McMullen," he called. "Is Wertz off on one of his fishing trips, or will I find him in town?"

"If it's your hair you're thinking about, come over here and sit down," Mrs. McMullen said. "Who do you think takes care of Ken's hair?"

"But, Mrs. McMullen —"

"Come over and take this chair — while I'm in the mood," Mrs. McMullen said.

The morning passed slowly. Twice, McMullen stopped by at the house. Neither time did he have an interesting report. Sam Holloway hadn't appeared in town, nor any of his men. Two ranchers from the east valley and another from Pueblo Mesa had shown up. But the man from Pueblo Mesa hadn't been Talbot.

"Jest take it easy," McMullen advised. "I'd reckon Sam Holloway won't hit town until midafternoon. Might be later. The Talbots could get in sooner. You think you got to see Susan?"

"I want to see her, sure," Linus answered. "Why not?"

"You want me to bring her here?"

"If you can."

"What'll I say to Weller Talbot? You know, I always liked Weller. But sometimes I just ain't sure about him. He puzzles me. It just came to me the other day that never, long as I been sheriff, has Weller gone with me on a posse."

"I suppose others haven't gone with you," Linus said.

"Yeah. Maybe so. Anyhow, if the Talbots get in afore Sam Holloway, I'll have a talk with Weller — and then bring Susan here."

"That would be fine," Linus said.

At noon, McMullen and Ken came home for dinner. Then, as soon as he could finish his meal, McMullen left. Up to then, neither Holloway nor the Talbots had appeared in town.

Ken took more time with his meal. He closed the store for the noon hour. Anyhow, he hadn't been awfully busy. Seed, grain, fertilizers, farm implements and supplies were a seasonal need. Sometimes, the store was left closed for days. Hoke Kenney, who owned it, did odd jobs in carpentry, to supplement his income.

"Didn't have anyone in the store all morning," Ken said. "Of course, this afternoon for a time I may be busy."

"But what did you do this morning?" Linus asked.

"I'm reading some books Judge Bellweather sent me. That keeps me busy."

"You stick to it," Linus said. "Don't let anything stop you from making it to Santa Fe. I haven't thought about it before, but I believe you'd be a good attorney."

Ken's eyes were dark, thoughtful, and although his body was rather chunky, his features weren't coarse. He had a high forehead, a straight nose and well-formed lips. The bulge of his jaw might have indicated stubbornness. He stood straight and he walked light-footed.

He spoke slowly. "Linus, I've been thinking. If Sam Holloway has done what we think, he would have tried to hide his crimes from as many of his men as he could."

"Yes, I think that's true," Linus nodded.

"So — some of his men know the truth about him, some don't."

"A good guess."

"The two men who came here with him, a man called Kansas and another called Durfree, seemed to be close to him. They might be expected to know the truth about him."

"That sounds reasonable.

"Then Katie might help us. Kansas and Durfree have both been to Katie's."

"Now that's interesting," Linus said. "Let me think about it."

They had been talking in the parlor, Mrs. McMullen in the kitchen, and now as Ken left, he left through the kitchen to speak to his mother. A moment later Linus noticed him through the window, cutting toward the main street. A damned nice young man. It ran across Linus' mind to wonder how Ken had known anything about Katie's. Then, rather ruefully, he remembered he had been only eighteen the first time he went to Katie's. So what the hell — maybe it wasn't strange at all that Ken knew his way around. And Katie's wasn't an evil place anyhow. The girls there, from what he knew and from what he had heard, followed some iron-clad rules Katie had established. A man who went to Katie's was separated from some of his money, but the price wasn't exorbitant. He wouldn't be clipped. And later, he wouldn't be blackmailed.

Linus walked back to the kitchen. He again helped with the dishes. Then, for the next hour he paced, feeling the pressure of the passing time. He didn't like it, cooped up inside. He had things to do. For one thing, he wanted to see Katie. He had a notion Katie would help him — if she could. Katie and his father had had some strange feeling for each other. Homer, too — Homer had been to Katie's many times — more often than he.

It was near two in the afternoon when he saw McMullen heading toward the house, and from the manner of his walk Linus could guess Sam Holloway was here. Instinctively, he checked his gun, and then shrugged and slid the gun back into its holster. Definitely, and no matter what happened, he didn't want to use his gun on Holloway — not yet. That would come — but only after he had learned the truth. That meant he had to control himself, not get impatient, not lose his head. When he faced Holloway he couldn't indulge in a wave of anger. He had to keep his mind active, sharp.

McMullen came in, nodded. "Holloway rode in 'bout ten minutes ago. Five men with him, but that's nothing unusual. Gave 'em time to settle down. They're at the Round Corral saloon."

"Who else is in the saloon?"

"Several men from the east valley. One or two from town. Enough so if you walk in Holloway will know you've got an audience. That's what we wanted."

"How long will he stay in the Round Corral?"

"Not long. He makes it a point not to hang around in the saloons. He'll work the street, go from store to store. Stop and talk here and there. This Holloway is a smart man — don't ever think he isn't. He's making friends, hand over fist."

"Then I'd better move," Linus said. "You get to the saloon. I'll follow you by two minutes."

"Good. If Holloway is about ready to leave, I'll stop him."

"What about the Talbots? I mean, did Susan —"

McMullen looked away. "They got here, but the way things worked out —"

"You mean, Holloway got here about the same time. That's all right. I can see Susan later."

McMullen nodded, waved to his wife and turned back toward town, and Mrs. McMullen said, "Linus, don't hurry. Never hurry."

"I'll try to remember that," Linus said.

He hitched up his pants, touched his holster and got his hat. Then he ran his fingers through his hair and remembered the shears snipping around his ears and he glanced at Mrs. McMullen. "I feel better, sure know I look better. Again, thanks a lot."

She smiled suddenly, a thin, little woman, getting old but holding her years amazingly well. A kind and pleasant woman, proud of her husband and her son —

50

and undoubtedly she had a lot to do with what kind of people they were.

He waved to her, making the wave a salute, and turned to the door and stepped outside.

He angled for the main street, cutting across a back yard, around one house and between two more. He didn't hurry, but he didn't delay either. On the way to the saloon he hoped he wouldn't meet anyone. He didn't want to have to stop and he didn't want to have to explain why he couldn't stop.

The route he took kept him off the main street until he was almost opposite the Round Corral saloon. And that far he was lucky; that far he met no one. As he hit the main street, however, and crossed toward the saloon, Sol Drews came out of his store, saw him and gasped. And then he called. "Hey, Linus! Linus! Wait a minute."

"Can't right now," Linus shouted back. "I'll stop in and see you later."

He noticed someone else as he was crossing the street. Susan and Jean. They were down at the corner of the hotel, another woman with them. Probably the mother of the girls. Jean waved, but he scarcely saw her. The one good look he had was directed at Susan. Tall, slender, straight, her head lifted, she was wearing a light-colored, summery dress, and a wide straw hat. A splash of flowers adorned the hat. She didn't wave, but then she wouldn't. She was more dignified, more adult than Jean.

Damnit, Linus wanted to see her — but that had to wait. He moved on, aware of two other men in front of the stage office, watching him. And to avoid the possibility of being delayed, he hurried, came to the door to the Round Corral saloon and pushed inside.

For part of a minute, probably, no one but McMullen noticed him — and that was natural for there was no reason for anyone to have been watching the door. That brief space of time gave Linus the opportunity to adjust his eyes to the shadowy interior of the saloon. It wasn't a large place, with its closed-off back room and a side room to a passageway leading to the rear and an outhouse. The bar stood opposite the side door and near the back room were two tables, often used for card games. There were several ceiling lanterns but none were on now, and the only light in the room this afternoon came from two soap-frosted windows in the front, and another on the side. In the winter, a stove stood in the rear of the room, but for the summer it had been stored away somewhere.

Linus had stopped just inside the door. He scanned the room, noticing three men playing black jack at one of the tables, and glancing at those at the bar — seven men. Two were ranchers from the east valley. With them was the smithy who lived here in town. That left the sheriff and three other men: Holloway and probably two of his companions. Linus had seen Holloway at the Coleman ranch, when he made his night trip to see who was there. He had seen him again riding up to Talbot's on Pueblo Mesa. A big, thick-bodied man, tall and heavy. He had a full face, the cheeks almost puffy, a square jaw fading into a corded, bull-like neck. Not a young man, but not old either. And not unattractive in appearance. He dressed well and looked neat. He was a man who might easily impress a woman.

About the other two men, Linus wasn't sure. He might have seen them at the Coleman ranch, but he couldn't be certain. One was thin, tall, young, freckled and had rusty hair. The other was more chunky and older. His dark jowls made him look unshaved. As he swung around and saw Linus he stiffened, and moved his right hand close to his holstered gun.

There had been a murmur of muted conversation in the air as Linus came in, but that was abruptly interrupted by McMullen's cry: "Why, look who's here. Linus Coleman! Where the hell did you come from?"

The others at the bar swung around to look at him, and Holloway and the thin fellow stiffened, just as the chunky man had done. For an instant, then, if Linus had given any sign of reaching for his gun, he would have died swiftly. He was sure of that. Sam Holloway and his two companions were trigger-edged. At even the hint of trouble, they would go for their guns.

But carefully, Linus made no move toward his. Instead, he raised one hand to push back his hat. The other he waved to McMullen. He called, "Hello there, Sheriff. Thought you knew where I been. Up in the Blacks, looking for gold. Wasn't very lucky."

Under normal circumstances, almost certainly someone would have made a crack about his search for gold. But nothing like that happened this afternoon. McMullen spoke again, and he sounded relieved. "By

God, Linus, I'm sure glad to see you. There's been a rumor going around that you were dead."

"Nope, not yet," Linus said. "In fact, I feel pretty good."

"I suppose you know about your folks," McMullen said. "I mean, about how they sold the ranch and moved out."

Linus frowned and shook his head. "No, I didn't know about that — until just the other day. Ran into two men in the mountains. They said father had sold out. I was sure as hell surprised. Came here to find out."

"You mean, Frank didn't send you any word?"

"Nope. None that I got."

Holloway spoke for the first time. "Didn't I explain about that, Sheriff?"

"Don't remember you did," McMullen said.

Linus was watching Holloway. The man was still on guard, still tense. He was watching Linus and his gun hand was free, but his voice, as he spoke, was pleasant, unhurried.

"It was like this," he was explaining. "Mr. Coleman and I talked about his son — the one on a gold hunt up in the mountains. But the trouble was, no one knew which part of the mountains he was in."

"Father knew where I went," Linus said bluntly, and that was true.

Holloway shrugged. "Then he must have forgot."

"My brother Homer also knew where I was going."

Holloway's eyes had narrowed and his face had tightened. But he didn't break into anger. "Maybe you're right. No skin off my nose. As I remember it, your folks said they didn't know how to reach you. Maybe they forgot or maybe not. Anyhow, you got word."

"Yes, I got word," Linus said.

He moved forward, spoke briefly to the east valley ranchers and to the smithy, and called to the bartender, asking for a beer. He crowded into a place between Holloway and McMullen. That put Holloway's companions on the other side of him, where they couldn't immediately support him.

"Where did your folks go?" McMullen asked.

Linus took a sip of his beer. He shook his head slowly. "You know, I can't figure it out. I didn't think father or Homer ever would leave the Rhymer Valley. Can't figure where they might have gone. It ain't realistic that they went. You know —"

"What?"

"I got a funny feeling they're still around — that they never left the valley."

"But where could they be?"

"Don't know," Linus said. "I'm gonna think about it. Yep, I sure am."

"You mean you're staying here — in the valley?"

"You bet I am."

"Found a place to stop?"

"No hurry about that."

Holloway touched his arm. "We spoke a moment ago, Coleman, but I didn't meet you properly. I'm Sam Holloway, who bought your father's ranch."

Linus swung sideways and nodded. He didn't smile. His eyes were steady, hard on Holloway's face.

"I just wondered," Holloway said. "You said you met two men in the mountains, and found out from them about your father. I wonder if those men could have been the two who came here looking for work. Tried 'em, but had to fire 'em."

"They had names," Linus said. "Lou Finney was one. The other was Ned Wilson."

"I reckon they won't be back."

"No," Linus said. "They won't be back."

Holloway's eyes showed a sudden flash of anger, but that was all. The man had good control of himself. He took a deep breath. "I been wondering about the Blacks. I'd like to go there sometime. If I was to follow the river —"

"That's the way I usually went — up the river. And coming back, I usually stopped at De Sellum's. Course, that's your place now."

"I had a man there, taking care of the place. Name was Shattuck. Maybe you met him."

"Sure. I met him," Linus said. "Quick on the trigger."

"But not quick enough."

"No," Linus said. "Not quick enough."

The man looked away. He had asked some questions, and he had been answered. He had guessed Finney and Wilson had been killed. Now he knew who was responsible. He must have guessed about Shattuck, too. Now he knew for sure. And probably his companions had guessed the truth also.

56

Then, suddenly, he had a chance to meet them. Holloway backed off from the bar and said, "Coleman, if you're going to be around, I'd like you to know Kansas and Al Durfree, who work with me. If you ever drop by at your old home, and I'm not there, Kansas or Al Durfree can look after you."

Linus nodded soberly to the two men. Judging by Holloway's nod, Kansas was the tall, thin, rusty-headed man, and Al Durfree was the shorter, older and uglier one. Linus didn't speak to them, but looked back at Holloway, and said, "Why, that's very nice of you, Holloway. But I suppose you'll be quite busy."

"Yes, I'll be busy," Holloway said.

"Too busy, of course, to spend much time on Pueblo Mesa."

The man blinked, took a quick breath. It hit Linus that he had been offensively plain as to what he knew and what he meant to say — that he had, in effect, just ordered Holloway to stay away from Susan. That might have brought on an explosion, but it didn't. Holloway rode the moment. He showed Linus a frosty smile and nodded. "We must see more of each other, Coleman. Drop over to the ranch, any time."

"Thanks," Linus answered. "Keep my room as it is. I might even want to move back home."

The smile, which wasn't a smile, stayed on Holloway's face. He waved casually with his arm and started for the door, motioning to Kansas and Al Durfree to follow him.

CHAPTER
FIVE

The wind seemed to be blowing harder when Sam Holloway stepped out into the street. And the clouds seemed darker. He looked up, realizing they did need more rain, but he didn't want it this afternoon, or this evening. He didn't look forward to a long ride in the rain.

That observation, however, slid in and out of his mind quickly and the real reason for his throbbing anger took his attention. He knew he didn't look worried on the surface. If some woman came by, right now, he would be able to touch his hat, smile and say something pleasant. That scene, back there in the saloon, had been a tough one to carry off. He would have liked to whip up his gun and use it on Linus Coleman. On the sheriff, too, if he had tried to interfere. But he had learned a long time ago that a man had to control his anger. There was nothing wrong with anger. It was a good, solid emotion, but if it got out of hand it could make a fool of a man. It could destroy him, and Sam Holloway wasn't ready to be destroyed.

Al Durfree spoke under his breath. "Lemme go back in there an' take him, Sam. I could start a fight, easy."

"No. Not yet," Sam said sharply. "And not that way."

"He knows too much," Durfree muttered.

"What the hell does he know? Nothing. Not a damned thing. He's guessing, sure. But who cares about that?"

"You mean, we're gonna let him have the run of the valley?"

Sam shook his head. "No. Not that. Gimme a little time to think. Al, you and Kansas stick together. Try the other saloon, and if Coleman comes in, move out. Keep away from him."

"He'll think we're scared," Durfree growled.

"That isn't important. Keep away from him. Did you hear me, Kansas?"

"Sure, I heard you," Kansas said. And then he made one of his rare observations. "When I see a rattlesnake, I stomp on him. Ain't a good plan to cuddle him."

"It's a cinch I won't cuddle him," Sam said.

He swung away and moved up the street, passed two women he had met in church and touched his hat, offering them a smile. The wind slapped at him, kicking up dust, and something got in his eye, nearly blinding him. He moved to the scanty protection of the doorway of the barbershop. Then a moment later he backed in, a hand covering one eye, the other watering.

"Something in your eye?" a voice asked. "Take my chair. Let's see if I can't help."

The voice sounded like that of Paul Wertz, who ran the shop. He caught Sam's arm, led him to the barber chair, and put a warm pack over both eyes. Then a minute later Wirtz was probing the painful eye, removed something with a twist of damp cloth and said, "There you are. Bit of sand. The eye will sting for a time, but that's all."

"Do you have a drink here anywhere?" Sam asked.

"Nope. Don't use it," Wirtz replied. "But you can get to the Round Corral or to Barlow's, easy."

"Let me stay here — until I get my breath."

"Stay long as you want to," Wirtz said. "For me, business is never rushing."

Sam leaned back in the barber's chair. He closed his eyes and concentrated on the problem of what to do about Linus Coleman. The day before, when they found the horses which had belonged to Lou Finney and Ned Wilson, and the bundles of personal belongings in the saddlebags, Sam had realized what must have happened up in the mountains. A little while later, when Shattuck was discovered in the De Sellum ranch house, shot to death, he knew whom to blame. Then, in another bit of bad luck, when Bern Jorgensen, fooling around with that girl in the darkness, and not on his toes, took a hell of a beating, getting several of his ribs broken, Holloway added that victory to the others won by Linus Coleman. The man had come back to the valley, must have guessed what happened to his folks, and had kicked back hard.

But Linus' successes had been up in the mountains, where he must have been just lucky — at De Sellum's, where Shattuck might have been trapped — and in the darkness near Talbot's, when Jorgensen had been jumped from behind. Look at it in that way, and Linus hadn't done so much — just a man riding the breaks.

60

Put him up against a real gun like Kansas, or Al Durfree, or Rupe Singer, and he wouldn't have a whisper of a chance. Why in hell was he worrying?

"Sure blowing out there in the street," the barber was saying. "You know, seeing a man through the dust can fool you. A little while ago I thought I saw Linus Coleman, 'cross the street."

"You did," Sam said. "Met him just a few minutes ago."

"Well, what do you know! So he didn't go with his folks."

"I reckon not. He said he'd been in the Blacks, prospecting. What's he like, Wertz?"

Wertz shrugged. "Nice young man. Not much like his father, or his brother Homer. They were real fire-eaters, brawlers. Good on the range, too, from what I heard. I mean, they could work, handle a job, then put in a full night drinking, raising hell. Carl McMullen sure had his hands full of them. He liked 'em, but every now and then he had to throw 'em in jail. They never fussed about it. And you know, people liked 'em. That is, if Frank Coleman or his son made any trouble, they paid for it. No arguments."

"But Linus is different?"

"Sure is. Don't think Linus ever got in a fight. Never did much drinking. Maybe his girl is responsible — Susan Talbot. Maybe you've met her."

Sam grinned wryly. Sure he had met Susan. He had been out with her last night, and if she belonged to Linus Coleman, she had shown him a funny kind of faithfulness. When he had kissed her she hadn't held back a bit. And she hadn't been fussy about keeping her blouse buttoned up. In fact, if they hadn't been interrupted by Talbot's excited calls when he found Jorgensen unconscious, he might have rolled Susan in his blanket. But that was in prospect next time he saw her. And to hell with Linus! The nerve of the man — to order him to keep off of Pueblo Mesa!

"With his folks gone, what do you think Linus will do?"

"Most likely, he won't stay here," Wirtz said. "I'd guess he'll follow his family. Course he might take Susan with him."

Sam nodded slowly. That was it, surely. Arrange it so Linus would follow his folks. Plant the idea Wertz had suggested, and then look after Linus out on the range — away from town, with no witnesses around. It shouldn't be any trouble at all, particularly in view of what he had learned. Linus was no fighter. If he had any guts at all he wouldn't have been shooting off his mouth in the saloon. He would have gone for his guns.

Sam got out of the chair and moved to the door. But he didn't step outside immediately. Three hunched riders, bundled against the wind, were heading up the street toward the livery. One was a woman in a divided skirt and leather jacket, Indian made, fringed and beaded, and wearing a brightly colored scarf. The other two riders were Rupe Singer and Turk Kiley. Rupe was something special — tops with his gun, and a problem in another way.

"Hey, isn't that your sister out there?" Wertz asked.

"Yes, my sister," Sam said — but that was a lie.

"Nice girl," Wertz said.

"Yes, a very nice girl," Sam said — and that was another lie.

Glory, whom he had introduced to Orotown and the Rhymer Valley, was a woman he had picked up in El Paso. He had brought her here just for the company, and if she had stayed out of sight, as he had expected, she wouldn't have been any problem. In bringing her he had told himself he was the kind of man who needed the companionship of a woman. But establishing himself here, he had to be very circumspect, very honorable. So he had brought her as his sister. Eventually, of course, he could easily send her packing.

But things hadn't worked out that way. Two complications came up. Glory took to the role of sister, all right, and promoted it. After they moved into the Coleman ranch, she took one of the separate bedrooms, and made it her own. A Mexican and her daughter, brought in as servants, became her personal attendants. And after a time she started ordering the men around, demanding small services, establishing her position. She had some help in this — that was the other complication. Rupe Singer had become her ally. Rupe was old and ugly and he limped badly from some ancient wounds. Pain from those injuries, always racking his body, twisted his face into bitter lines. And twisted his mind, too — Rupe had grown vicious, sadistic, cruel. He was as dangerous as they came. Neither Kansas nor Al Durfree wanted to challenge Rupe Singer.

A few weeks ago Sam could have sent Glory away. Today he couldn't. She would refuse, appealing to Rupe Singer — and what that might lead to Sam didn't know. At any rate, until things were quieter and until he felt more assured of his place in the valley, he didn't want to risk any trouble at home. He would ride his uneasiness about Glory and Rupe, just as he had to ride out any storm, slide through it until the weather turned better. And anyhow, Rupe, whatever his relationship with Glory, hadn't crowded him out of her life. He was still welcome in her bedroom, where she was one of the best.

"Glory!" Wertz said. "Nice name for a girl. Fits her."

Sam smiled crookedly. He wondered what Wertz would say if he knew Glory was a hard thirty, could swear better than most men, and outdrink them, too. She had sandy hair, which she could pile high, curl, and make mighty handsome — but at breakfast she looked as frowzy as hell. She had a flabby roll of flesh around her stomach, too, but it didn't show under her corset, which she always wore, even when she went horseback riding.

"Got some things to do," Sam said. "Thanks for the operation on my eye."

He pushed outside and headed for the hotel. Women from the range country often gathered there, to wait for their menfolk. Susan might be among them. He had seen her earlier on the street, with her sister and mother. There wasn't much point in seeing her in town, but girls liked attention, and he wanted to arrange a meeting some place where they wouldn't be interrupted.

When Linus crossed the street and disappeared in the Round Corral saloon, Jean spoke to her sister. "At least, you could have waved. If I were in your shoes —"

"Don't you wish you were," Susan said, and laughed.

To Jean the laugh was a slap in the face. It brought color to her cheeks. How Susan had learned of her interest in Linus she didn't know. Probably it had been obvious, but then, that was her way.

"There are some things I still must do," Mrs. Talbot said. "Why don't you two girls go to Mrs. Wadsworth's? When your father and I are finished with our shopping, we'll drive by there and pick you up."

The Wadsworths lived in a house back of the main street, and Jean searched for a reason not to leave the center of town. Before she could find one, however, Susan managed it. "I want to see Molly Carver about a new hat. After that, I'll come back to the hotel lobby."

"I'll stay with Susan," Jean added quickly.

"I suppose that's all right," Mrs. Talbot said.

As she moved away, Susan looked at Jean with narrowed eyes. "Well, Miss Tag-along, I don't know whether I like this or not."

"I just didn't want to be sent somewhere," Jean said. I don't intend to tag along. When you meet Linus — what's the matter?"

Susan was shaking her head. "I'm not sure that will be possible. I mean — have you looked at Father lately?"

"What about him?"

"You're not a very sensitive person, are you?"

"What's sensitive? You mean, if Sam Holloway brings a man to see me, I'm supposed to go out with him and let him paw me, just so father doesn't get embarrassed?"

"That's putting it crudely. Father is worried. He doesn't want trouble. And I don't either. If I can make things easier just by seeing Mr. Holloway —"

"And how about Linus?"

"Linus doesn't have to know. And, Jean, if you tell him —"

Jean was staring at his sister, with an honesty Susan didn't like. Jean spoke slowly. "I just wonder if you're not enjoying yourself. Last night, for instance — what happened between you and Sam Holloway?"

Susan laughed suddenly. "Nosy! Don't you wish you knew?"

"I can guess," Jean snapped.

That made Susan angry. "Nothing happened. Don't be foolish. And don't turn your sheep eyes on Linus. He won't even notice you."

Jean looked away. She was afraid Susan was right about that. Linus would never look at her — really look at her. She was the little sister, and of course the way she usually dressed didn't help her — in levis and blouse around the house, in a plain, unattractive dress when she went to town, long and dark, and with no fancy trimmings. Susan, in contrast, was wearing a blue and white cotton print, trimmed with ribbons, with a lace yoke at the throat. It was almost indecently tight over her breasts. And she did have nice breasts.

"I don't think I want to see Molly," Susan was saying. "I'm going to wait in the hotel lobby. Why don't you see Molly and have her make a dress for you? Father would pay for it, and that dress you're wearing is horrible."

Jean smiled quickly. This was the first time Susan had ever shown any interest in her appearance. It gave her a good feeling. She started to answer, but then a sudden suspicion crossed her mind. If she went to Molly's, she would be kept there, being fitted and talked to, and while that went on, Susan would be waiting in the hotel. Not alone, but at least unattended.

"Go ahead," Susan said. "Have Molly make you a grown-up dress. It's time Father spent a little money on you."

Jean was satisfied, now, Susan was sending her away. She meant to meet someone — Linus or Sam, most likely. It wasn't like her to be worried about Jean's appearance. But she didn't argue. She said, "Yes, maybe I should get a dress."

She crossed the street and started in the direction of the dressmaker's, but as she reached the grocery she hesitated, then stepped inside. Sol Drews had waved to her from the window, and as she came in he said, "Hello there, Jean. You see him — Linus Coleman?"

"Yes, we saw him from the corner," Jean said.

"He went in the Round Corral. Holloway was there, and a couple of his men. Ain't heard nothing. No shooting. I reckon some of us have been talking out of turn."

"What do you mean?" Jean asked, but she thought she knew.

"If Linus is in there with Holloway, couldn't be nothing wrong with the way Holloway got the Coleman ranch. Hey, there's Sam Holloway now, leaving the saloon. Two of his men with him. Kansas and Al Durfree."

Jean turned to the window and looked across toward the saloon. She noticed Holloway and the two men talking, then after a few moments, Kansas and Al Durfree headed up the street. Sam Holloway went the other way, toward the hotel. But he didn't go to the hotel. He stopped at the barbershop.

Sol Drews turned toward her. "Hey, Jean. What are you doing?"

She smiled. "Just waiting for my folks."

"Then, mind looking after the store for a minute? Never very busy this time of the day. If anyone comes in, have them wait. I'd like to — I want to see Linus."

Jean nodded. "I'll watch the store."

She was still smiling as he hurried across the street, and it gave her a warm feeling to realize that Sol Drews, like almost everyone in town, was really very fond of Linus. Maybe he didn't have the colorfulness of his father and brother, but he must have other qualities people liked. Her father had said once that Linus was one of the few people he knew who could understand other people's problems, and Susan had mentioned he was too easy with people. That could be a good trait or a bad one.

Standing at the window, looking into the street, she noticed three riders heading up toward the livery stable, and one interested her: the woman — Glory Holloway, Sam Holloway's sister. From what Jean had heard, she was rather young, extremely attractive, an expert rider and a good person. Her mother had been delighted to meet her in church. Mrs. Talbot had characterized her as a fine Christian woman — sweet and gentle. But only a week ago, here in Orotown, she had been watching Glory Holloway when Katie came out of the bank. Parlor House Katie. She had turned in the direction of Glory, and when Glory saw her she stiffened, turned pale, then quickly ducked into the hotel.

Whatever that look on Glory's face meant, Jean was interested.

Glory and the two men riding with her, men who worked for her brother, continued up the street and a moment later Sam Holloway came out of the barbershop. This time he continued on to the hotel, and entered the lobby. *And Susan was in the lobby*. Of course, a hotel lobby was a public place and if Susan and Sam Holloway met there, it could look accidental. But Jean couldn't help feeling uneasy.

She shifted her attention to the Round Corral saloon. Three men were coming out — Mr. Drews, Mr. McMullen and Linus. Her eyes centered on him quickly. Tall, thin, laughing about something. Just another young man, not too well dressed, not too handsome. Why did she have to worry about him? Surely, in this wide country there ought to be a dozen young men who could attract her attention.

The three men entered the store, and Sol Drews gestured toward her. "See, I told you I had a helper. Jean Talbot."

"Hello, Jean," Linus said. "Where's Susan?"

She answered promptly, not even hesitating over the lie. "I don't know where she is, Linus. Possibly with mother at the Emporium."

"I want to see her before you folks leave," Linus said, and then he drew her aside and lowered his voice. "Any trouble last night after I left?"

She shook her head. "Not very much. I told father what had happened. He — he sent me in the house, went out and got Mr. Jorgensen, carried him in, and then he shouted for Mr. Holloway."

"Where was Holloway?"

"I — I think Susan and Mr. Holloway took a walk. That is —" She had to say it that way. There was no way to avoid part of the truth.

"That's all right," Linus said, and he seemed to be growling the words. "I'll look after Holloway soon as I can. You tell Susan — no, I'll tell her. Did you tell Holloway who was responsible?"

"I told father, but father didn't tell. He just said it was some man. And Sam didn't ask any questions. I think he knew you were there."

Linus nodded. He turned to look through the window, then said, "Jean, think you could find your sister?"

70

She answered, frowning, "Yes, I think so."

She turned away, suddenly bitter. Linus hadn't even noticed her. But then with Susan in town she should have expected nothing else. There was no point in not being honest with herself.

"When you folks leaving town?" McMullen asked.

"I don't know exactly," Jean said. "But I think father will want to leave very soon."

"Not until I've seen Susan," Linus said.

The sheriff looked at Linus, then looked away, and he was hesitant. "I talked to Susan earlier. Didn't tell you what she said, 'cause I didn't want to see you upset afore you talked to Holloway. I reckon it's like this, Linus. On account of her father and until we settle things, she doesn't want to see you."

Linus had straightened. The hurt look on his face made Jean angry at her sister. He spoke slowly. "I don't believe it. I don't think Susan —"

McMullen cleared his throat. He said, "Jean, ain't it a fact that Holloway's been pestering your folks?"

She nodded, watching Linus. She couldn't speak.

"Let's use our heads," McMullen said. "Ain't gonna hurt any to leave the Talbots out of it till we get things lined up. Way things are, you're not going to have any time for sparking, anyhow, the next few days."

"I suppose you're right," Linus said, but there was a dead sound in his voice.

Jean swung away. She couldn't stand to hear any more. If the sheriff kept on talking, he would make a heroine of Susan — describe her as a brave, courageous girl, sacrificing her virtue on the altar of her family's safety. But that wasn't the way it was at all. If she really wanted to, Susan could arrange to see Linus. Even if it had to be a secret meeting, it could be set up. In her place, she would do something like that.

She started down the street, against the wind, her head bowed. Then suddenly she bumped up against someone, reeled away, caught her balance, and looked at the man she had run into. He was nearly as big as Sam Holloway. A young-old man, thick-bodied, tall, a grin on his ruddy face. But even the grin couldn't make the man look pleasant. A name jumped into her mind, identifying him — Turk Kiley, who worked with Holloway. Another man was with him, a smaller man, stooped, aging and ugly. Rupe Singer.

Kiley stretched his hand toward her. "Sorry, ma'am. Didn't mean to bump you. But I been sorta wanting to meet you. Now if you and me —"

She snapped out her answer. "If I had a gun, I'd use it. Right now. Get out of my way."

The man laughed provokingly, but stepped aside. Jean hurried on, and she should have felt better. She had just asserted her independence rather well. For some strange reason, however, she didn't feel better. In fact, she was on the verge of tears.

CHAPTER
SIX

Linus moved around town. He stopped and spoke to twelve or fifteen people he knew, some of them ranchers, some people who lived in town. It was no accident that wherever he went McMullen wasn't far off. This was just a bit of insurance. Linus might not need it, but at least it was a steadying influence to know he wasn't alone.

In the process, Linus got a good look at some of Holloway's men: Kansas, who seemed to have no other name, Al Durfree, Rupe Singer and Turk Kiley. Linus also managed to meet Sam's sister, Glory. And his reactions to her were conflicting. She seemed pleasant, but her eyes were sharp and hard. In addressing him, her words were correct, but her voice was sultry, intimate, like the dare of a coquette. It was hard to guess her age, but Linus thought she might be thirty or older. There were thin lines at the corners of her eyes and around her mouth. Her throat was wrinkled, too.

"Linus Coleman," she said, putting out her hand. "You're the younger son — the one who was up in the mountains digging gold."

"Looking for gold is a better description," Linus said. "I didn't find much."

She laughed. "That's too bad. I could very easily get interested in a man who came to me round-shouldered from the gold he was carrying."

"Is that the only requirement?" Linus asked.

"Stay around and find out."

"I think I will."

"Come by sometime. After all, you should have the right to visit your old home."

They were in the hotel lobby and it was late in the afternoon. A number of others were around, but chiefly Linus noticed Kansas, Turk Kiley and Rupe Singer. They stood grouped together, watching him and Glory — and McMullen wasn't far away. Kansas, tall, thin, rusty-haired and freckled, wore a sardonic grin. Turk Kiley, big and hefty, was scowling. But it was Rupe Singer he noticed in particular. In the ugly, warped figure of Rupe Singer he could feel a sudden, burning hatred. It struck across the room at him the way a cold draft of air can sweep across a chamber. Linus shifted uneasily. If he was right in what he sensed, it puzzled him. A man didn't hate on sight. There had to be a reason for it — and he couldn't find it. He was sure he had never seen Rupe Singer in his life.

He touched his hat, smiled at Glory and turned away. Then in Sol Drews' store, he replenished his tobacco, rolled a smoke and lit it.

McMullen, who had followed him, spoke from the door. "They're not gonna try anything — least while it's light."

"Where's Holloway?" Linus asked.

74

"In the bank, I think. Don't know what he wants with Henry Nugent. Find out later."

"What will Holloway do with the rest of the day — and the evening?"

"He and his men and Glory will eat in the hotel dining room. Then there's a dance at the town hall. There'll be a fair crowd. Sam Holloway will dance with every woman on the floor. He'll show no favors. He'll flatter the older women especially. A few more months and he'll be the most popular man in the valley. He keeps his men in line, too."

"Does he bring his men to church?"

McMullen laughed shortly. "No. He doesn't go that far. But he'll be in to church tomorrow himself. And he'll bring his sister. A couple of his men will ride in and hit the saloons. You know, I've noticed Sam Holloway is never alone. Got someone with him wherever he goes. Right now, Al Durfree is with him in the bank."

"Sam does watch himself," Drews said. "I was talking to Katie the other day, asked her what she thought of him, and she told me straight off that she didn't know him — that he never had been to see her. Said most of his men had been in, but not Sam."

"That reminds me," Linus said. "I've been meaning to talk to Katie."

"You might learn something from her or you might not," McMullen said. "Katie can be damned close-mouthed when she feels like it. Sometimes she helps me, sometimes she doesn't."

"Then let me try her," Linus said. "I don't know why it was, but my father had a funny feeling about Katie. He seemed to like her."

"Do myself," McMullen said. "In her own way she's straight. Used to be a looker, years ago. Came from Chicago. That's about all I know about her."

"Why don't I see her now?" Linus suggested.

The sheriff shook his head. "Sometimes you see Katie out on the street in the afternoon, but it's not until after dark that she comes to life. Thinks better then. We'll try her then."

Katie's Parlor House was around the corner from the bank, its back door convenient to the Round Corral saloon. So far as that was concerned, however, the back door was convenient to anyone who cut back of the main street.

Once the back entrance had been lighted by a lamp just inside the glass-paneled door. But one evening several years ago a man had been shot to death at Katie's back door, and the murderer, hiding in the shadows, had been helped by the lamplight. Since then the rear entrance hadn't been lighted. A man had to find the door, knock and be admitted in darkness. A few complained, but Katie said if a man was too drunk to find the door he might as well stay out anyway.

Linus and Carl McMullen knocked on Katie's back door just after dark. One of her girls admitted them and led them to the lighted parlor room, where she looked frightened when she saw who they were. She was a thin, dark-haired girl, and rather pretty. When

76

McMullen said they wanted to see Katie, she still seemed worried. But she took them to the woman's sitting room.

Katie joined them almost immediately, and in spite of the dim lamplight, it was bright enough for Linus to get a good look at her. A big woman, too fleshy, and so powdered and painted it wasn't easy to guess what was underneath. She reeked with perfume, too. Her hair was curled and piled high on her head. Her face was puffy and she was no longer young. But then again she might not be very old. Linus wouldn't have risked guessing at her age.

Her greeting was pleasant. "Hello, Carl. Sometimes it's nice to see you. And this is Linus? Where did your folks move to, Linus?"

"I don't know," Linus said. "That's one of the things I want to talk to you about."

She motioned to some chairs. "Sit down. What are you hinting at?"

"I don't think Father sold his ranch. I think Father and Homer were killed — murdered."

She looked at McMullen. "What do you think, Carl?"

"I don't know what to think," McMullen said. "I've got a feeling something's wrong. I smell trouble."

She sat down abruptly, her lips working. Then she stared at Linus and said, "I liked your father. Knew him years ago, after your mother died — for a while knew him too well, but we both got over it. I didn't care too much for Homer. He was a little rough. What are you like? Do you feel too good for this place?"

"I've been here," Linus said.

"Not for a long time. Anyhow, it's your father I'm worried about now. Sam Holloway's never come near us."

"His men come here."

She nodded slowly. "I'll talk to the girls. If I learn anything, chances are I'll let you know. As I said, I rather liked Frank Coleman."

McMullen stood up. "That's all we wanted, Katie. If you can help us —"

"See about that," Katie said, and she pointed at Linus. "What I'm wondering about is him. What's he like? Any son of Frank Coleman's ought to have a little blood in his veins."

"Where do you want me to spend it?" Linus grinned. "Here in your place?"

Katie's eyes brightened. "So you can talk back, huh? At least, that's something. Drop in some night, just to gab — when Carl isn't around."

"I might do that," Linus said.

"If I'm busy — and that happens — ask for Gail. I think you'd like her."

"I'll remember that."

"Maybe you will, maybe you won't," Katie said. "All right, get out. Nothing more to be said tonight."

Linus was smiling as they left. He said, "Mac, she's quite a character, isn't she?"

"She speaks her own mind, at least. And she's honest," McMullen said.

"Who's the girl Katie mentioned — Gail? Do you know her?"

"I've seen her. She hasn't been here long — maybe two months. In the early twenties, prettier than most. A rather tall girl, brown-haired, spirited. Or at least that's what I've heard. But most of Katie's girls are pretty decent."

They walked on, heading in the direction of the sheriff's home, talking about Katie and her girls and the uneasiness and strain McMullen could sense in town. It could be attributed, definitely, to Holloway and the men he had brought. A hard-looking crowd. They hadn't stepped out of line — yet. But they would. It was inevitable.

"Anyhow, that's enough talk," McMullen said. "You go on home, pile in bed on the couch. I want to check at my office."

"Go to bed this early?" Linus said.

"Why not? You may need it."

"Maybe I do," Linus admitted.

He continued on his way, switching his thoughts to a consideration of Susan. But even to think about her made him angry. Not angry at her, of course, but at her father and at the situation Weller Talbot couldn't control. Linus thought he knew exactly the way Susan felt. As he lined up the problem, Sam Holloway wasn't married, and looking around at the possibilities, he had noticed Susan. That had been inevitable. She was young, beautiful and seemed available. So he had started paying attention to her, and her father hadn't had the courage to get in the way. Actually, what Susan was doing she had to do, to protect her family, and what a rotten situation that was.

"By God, I wouldn't have taken it," Linus muttered, thinking of Weller Talbot, and smashing his fist into his palm. Then he started walking faster. He suddenly decided what to do with the rest of the evening.

He stopped at the sheriff's home, talked to Mrs. McMullen, explained where he was going, and told her to tell her husband not to worry. He knew Mac probably would, but he couldn't help that. Out in the barn he saddled up, and a few moments later he rode away, taking the north road from the edge of town. In an hour he was climbing to Pueblo Mesa and in another hour he reined up in sight of the Talbot ranch.

It was now rather late for a visit. No lights showed in the house. Linus pulled up at the springhouse, tied his horse there, and then walked across the field in the direction of the ranch buildings. Weller had a dog, he remembered, but maybe he was kept inside. At any rate, the dog didn't appear as he reached the yard, crossed to the house and circled toward the rear.

He knew the girls' window and he crept close to it. It was open slightly. He risked a low whisper. "Susan . . . Susan . . . it's Linus Coleman. Susan — wake up."

He heard no sounds from inside and he waited for a moment then tried again. This time someone inside stirred, and a shadowy figure came to the window.

"Susan!" he whispered. "Susan, it's Linus. Climb outside for a minute. I'll help you."

A low whisper reached him. "I'll get dressed. Wait for me."

80

Linus took a deep, satisfying breath. He nodded to himself. Everything was going to be all right. Susan hadn't changed. What had he been worrying about?

Above him, the window was raised higher. He looked up, and as the girl started to climb out he whispered, "Careful — I'm right here." He reached to help her.

She came down in his arms, which was all right, and the shadowy darkness didn't prevent him from finding her face, then her lips. He pulled her close, kissing her hungrily, and from the way she clung to him and the way she returned the kiss, he knew she was exactly where she wanted to be. He pulled slightly away to get a breath of air and he whispered, "Susan! Susan, I —"

He broke off suddenly, an impossible thought crossing his mind. Then in an instant he knew his suspicion was right. He had been tricked. This wasn't Susan. It was Jean who had been kissing him — kissing him just as she had the other evening. So well and thoroughly it made him shaky — but angry, too.

She must have sensed it. He heard her catch her breath, could feel her stiffen. She said, "Linus, I — that is — you didn't give me a chance to say who I was."

"Didn't I?" Linus said. "Why did you climb out here, anyhow? It was Susan I asked for."

"She's not here," Jean said. "That's what I came to explain."

"Not here! But where is she?"

"She stopped to spend the night with Ellie Aldrich."

"Back near town?"

Jean nodded. "Susan and Ellie are very good friends. But you already know that. Susan's stayed there before."

Linus was silent, and vaguely uneasy. Why couldn't Susan have sent a message to him? Ellie's brother could have carried him a note, and he would have been with Susan almost two hours ago. The Aldrich family had one of the clustering farms, just below Orotown.

Jean reached out, touched his arm. "Linus, I'm sorry. But when I saw you I didn't know Susan was going to spend the night with Ellie. And I didn't guess you meant to ride to the mesa."

"I just did it on impulse," Linus said.

"If it wasn't so late you could turn back, but it must be after ten."

"Yes, it would be after midnight before I got back," Linus admitted.

Jean spoke again. "You still mad at me, Linus?"

"I'm not mad at you," he said slowly. "I just don't know what to do about you. Do you go around kissing everyone else like you kissed me?"

"I almost never kiss anyone," Jean said. "With you it — it just happened."

"If you were just a little older —"

"I'm old enough."

He took a deep breath. The sudden temptation to reach out and take her in his arms was almost overpowering. Maybe she was as old as she thought. At least, when he had kissed her she had not been passive. But damn it, she was still Susan's sister — her little sister. That was the point he had to keep in mind.

82

She spoke slowly. "When I think about tonight I'll hate myself — for what I did. It wasn't nice."

"No, don't say that," Linus said. "We all step out of line now and then. One of the important things in life is to be able to get back on the right track."

"You mean, if I climb back through that window and if you walk away, we'll be getting on the right track."

Her voice had changed. She sounded amused. He couldn't see her face but he was suddenly sure her eyes were twinkling. And what did that mean? Damnit, this girl wasn't any little sister. She was uncomfortably wise.

He spoke gruffly. "We're just talking, and getting all mixed up. You better climb in the window, 'cause it's late. I've got to ride on, 'cause I've a long trip ahead."

"Back to town, Linus?"

"No. I want to see Erb Wylie, and Sunday morning might be a good time to see him."

She stiffened again. "You can't risk it, Linus. If you go to the ranch they'll — they'll kill you."

"Maybe not, Jean."

He scowled at her. What was he doing, calling her "Jean"? In the past he had called her "girl," and she had liked it.

She had moved closer and once more she put her hand on his arm. She sounded troubled. "Linus, I don't want to say the wrong things. I know you're going to have to take some chances. But to go to the ranch where Mr. Holloway — why don't you wait until the sheriff can go with you?"

"That would be too official — or maybe I should put it this way. On my own I won't be too hampered by the law. I can do things alone the sheriff wouldn't approve — like busting in a door or a window to search inside."

"You're going there now — to your father's ranch?"

"Yes — but I don't know when I'll try to reach Erb Wylie. Probably toward morning, or maybe after sunup. Depends. Are you going to church tomorrow morning?"

She nodded. "We usually do. Particularly since Susan will be at church with Ellie, we'll want to pick her up."

"Could you see Carl McMullen, or his son, or his wife? Give him word that I went to see Erb?"

He knew she was frowning. "That means you're worried you might not get back."

"Nope. I just want McMullen to know what I'm up to. Don't worry, Jean. I'll be so careful I may accomplish nothing. That's a failing of mine — to be too careful."

"I don't call it a failing. If I thought you were telling the truth, I'd sleep better."

"Then sleep sound as a winter bear."

"And wake up with my claws out, Linus?"

He laughed softly, "Just don't use them on me. Now I better help you up to your window."

Her voice changed, a provoking tone challenging him. "What would you do if I slipped and fell back in your arms? I could do that easily."

"Do that, and you get spanked," Linus said.

"You wouldn't dare!"

"Oh, yes, I would. Come on, now. Reach up."

Linus boosted her to the window and as she leaned inside, he shoved hard. From the sounds he heard, Jean spilled to the floor, and not too gently. Linus waited until her head and shoulders reappeared, staring down at him. She whispered angrily, "You did that on purpose. You — you treated me like a sack of grain. Just wait! I'll get even."

"You'll just get trouble with me," Linus said. "Next time, it's the spanking I threatened. That's a promise, girl."

"For a while you called me Jean."

"I looked at you again."

She sighed. "I just can't get grown up."

"It'll happen," Linus said. "And too swiftly. Then you never get to turn back to the nice days of your childhood. It's a greater loss than you realize."

He turned away, crossed the field to the dark mass of trees sheltering the springhouse, found his horse, mounted and rode south and west, toward the Rhymer Valley and his father's ranch — once called Coleman's, and now probably already being called Holloway's. Sam Holloway's. He had been remembering Jean. He wished to hell it could have been Susan, but if he had to miss her, at least her sister was colorful enough to be interesting. In fact, if he wasn't careful, he could get too interested in her. And the way she could kiss . . .

Still in the trees, Linus pushed Jean out of his mind and switched his thoughts to Holloway and everything that represented him: his sister — the men working for him — his position in the valley. So swiftly it was unbelievable, Holloway had taken an important place in the valley. If he ran into any trouble, he already had a crowd to stand behind him, for from his attitude he was winning friends in town. In a little while it might even be foolish to challenge him.

Linus reined up to roll a smoke. Then he rode on, concentrating on the possibilities which lay just ahead. Right now, very likely, Holloway, his sister and most of his men were in town. The dance would keep them late. It would be toward morning before they started home. Holloway, of course, wouldn't get much rest. Soon after he returned he would have to leave for church. He might even stay in town, to save the long ride.

McMullen had told him Holloway had close to a dozen men working the valley. And he would need that many, in view of the size of his operations. He might need even more riders. Some, like Kansas and Al Durfree, and Rupe Singer and Turk Kiley, had the appearance of a fighting force. Maybe they could do ranch work, but they didn't look like workers.

He was getting off the subject. What about tomorrow? What should he expect when he got to Holloway's? Again, from what McMullen had said, Erb Wylie didn't come to town very often. He might have been afraid to come, or he might have been ordered to stay home. At any rate, in all probability he would be able to find Erb at the ranch before the crowd from town got back.

Linus cut down from the mesa, and kept at a steady clip up the valley. It was a black night, not a time to hurry, but he knew the valley from end to end. This darkness would be more of a handicap to Holloway than it was to him. It was still windy, too, and possibly the wind would bring rain.

It was well after midnight when he reined up in the yard. No lights showed anywhere, and no one challenged him. Linus reined over to the corral. He swung to the ground, loosely tied his horse, and walked to the bunkhouse. When a crowd was in town, anyone might return at any time, care for his horse, and then head for the bunkhouse and a few hours of rest. He hadn't done anything about his horse, but in walking to the bunkhouse he was doing a very normal thing.

But what he did next wasn't so normal. Linus entered the bunkhouse, struck a match, found a table lamp and lit it. After that he drew his holster gun and scanned the room. In the double bunks he counted five recumbent figures. One was the man he wanted — Erb Wylie, thin, hawk-faced, whiskered, black-haired, in his late forties.

Another man, disturbed by the lamp, made a grumbling protest. "Damnit, cut out that light." He muttered profanely and rolled his face the other way.

Linus walked to where Erb was sleeping. He touched the man's shoulder and said, "Erb! Erb, wake up."

The man groaned, muttered unintelligibly, and raised one arm to push Linus away.

"Erb! Wake up," Linus said. "I want to talk to you."

He shook the man harder and this time the man awoke. He looked up, saw who was leaning above him, and caught his breath. Until that instant he had been groggy, but he wasn't groggy now. He was suddenly wide-awake, startled, frightened. He seemed to want to speak, but couldn't.

"On your feet, pull your boots on," Linus ordered, his voice low. "We're going to take a walk."

Finally the man could say something. He wagged his head from side to side. "No, Linus, please. I didn't —"

He didn't finish what he had started. He had abruptly run out of air. For the moment, Linus didn't say anything. He was watching the man who had been first to awaken, had protested the light, then had seemed to go back to sleep. But he hadn't gone to sleep. He was stirring again, changing position, pushing one of his arms under the pillow. That might not mean a thing, but Linus knew it could. More than half the men in an ordinary bunkhouse kept a gun under their pillows when they went to bed.

A man in an upper bunk was snoring. Two lay in deep sleep, and where Linus could watch them. The one partially awake — or maybe wholly awake — was two bunks over from Erb's. His back was this way, and he wasn't moving right now, but to Linus he seemed too rigid. He was a man with iron-gray hair, big shoulders, not young.

"Erb," Linus said, still under his breath. "On your feet. Reach for your boots and pull 'em on."

The man was perspiring. "No, Linus. I never —"

"You can tell me later — outside," Linus said.

He was holding his holster gun and he leveled it straight at Erb's face. It was so close Erb could have looked down the barrel. He sat up as Linus drew back

88

the gun, reached for his boots and pulled them on. He asked, "Where we — where we goin', Linus?"

"Don't worry about that," Linus said. "Get up and pull your pants on."

The man did, awkwardly and shakily, and breathing too fast. He was still perspiring.

"Now head for the door," Linus said.

He measured the distance to be covered — half a dozen steps. They had to walk that far to the door, and they were within a few seconds of it. But that man two bunks over definitely wasn't asleep. He had worked one arm under his body, one hand still under his pillow. In any minute, the man could rear up, and if he had a gun, he could try to get a shot off. And at the very least that would arouse the others.

Linus raised his voice just a little. He called, "Listen, fellow — if you try —"

That was as far as he got. The man two bunks over did just what he had feared, reared up in the air, twisting toward him. He had a gun under his pillow, and he was so anxious to use it he fired his first shot into the floor. He ripped a second into the bunk next to Erb's. His third shot might have reached Linus, but he didn't get a third shot. Linus fired back, dropped the man, and then stepped quickly toward the door.

He whipped out a harsh order. "Erb, open the door. And don't gimme any trouble."

Erb gulped, but said nothing. He fumbled with the door, opened it.

The three men who had been asleep were instantly awake. Maybe all three guessed who Linus was, and could figure what had happened. But more likely all three were dazed, startled and didn't know what to do. The gun Linus was waving from side to side might have helped. At least, it warned them to be careful.

"Stay in your bunks and you won't get hurt," Linus said. "Chase after us and you'll be sorry."

No one offered to speak. The man who had been shot was groaning. Linus risked a glance at him. He couldn't be sure how badly he had been hurt, but he could guess. He had aimed to drop the man. He might live — but the chances were on the other side.

"All right, Erb," Linus said. "We'll step outside and take our walk. Don't try to run."

Erb backed outside, and Linus followed. He closed the bunkhouse door.

CHAPTER
SEVEN

Linus wasted no time in getting away from the ranch, and he took Erb with him. Later, undoubtedly, Erb would get his walk, but to begin with they rode double, Erb using the saddle, Linus behind him. They struck south. In a few hours, as soon as it grew light, those at the ranch would be able to pick out his trail, but as black as it was, Linus didn't have to worry about immediate pursuit. He had a fair margin of safety. And it might rain. If it rained hard his trail would be washed out.

He really didn't think he needed the rain. The few hours he could have with Erb, between now and dawn, should be enough. Erb was frightened, shaky. To start with, he would lie — and all the way through, he would lie. But sticking to his falsehoods would be traces of the truth. At least, Linus would learn a few things from Erb Wylie.

Erb started talking. "Linus — Linus, I don't know what you're doin' this for. I ain't done nothin' wrong. Honest to God, I ain't."

"If you've done nothing wrong, then you've nothing to worry about," Linus answered.

"But — where we goin'?"

"We're just riding," Linus said. "Did you know Lou Finney and Ned Wilson?"

Erb spoke too quickly. "No, I didn't."

"They came to see me in the mountains — tried to finish me," Linus said. "I buried them. Course you knew Shattuck. I killed him, too. Then who was it I shot tonight — in the bunkhouse?"

"Art Deneen."

"Too bad," Linus said. "But I want you to think about it. I don't want to have to shoot you, Erb. But if I have to I'll do it, just like that."

He snapped his fingers, stared bleakly at the dark figure in the saddle just in front of him. This boasting he had been doing was a new experience, but if it would increase Erb's fears, it was worth it.

"You got no call to shoot me," Erb said. "You just say what you want me to do, and I'll do it."

"I want to know what happened to my father, my brother, Mike Bellows — just the story of what happened to my folks. You were there. You can tell me."

Erb shifted uneasily. "I don't know what to say."

"You'd better," Linus said. "If you want to live, you'd better know. Think about it. We got another hour of riding. Maybe several hours."

"Where we goin'?" Erb asked again.

"Maybe into the badlands," Linus said.

"But what we gonna go there for?"

"Just one reason," Linus said. "Down there in the badlands, under the shifting sands, is a good place to hide a body."

Erb raised his voice, sounding almost hysterical. "No, Linus. No — please. I'll tell you —"

"All right, we'll see about that," Linus said. "I'll ask one question. If you answer honestly, truthfully, you get a chance. What happened to my father?"

Erb Wylie stiffened, sucked in a sharp breath. "Linus, I don't know. Honest to God, I don't."

He was almost shouting, but he didn't keep it up. Linus whipped up his gun and smashed the barrel over Erb's head. He put the gun away, and steadied the man until he could rein up. Then he swung to the ground, pulled Erb down, and dumped him on the ground. He hobbled his horse, and walked back to where Erb was lying.

In a few minutes Erb Wylie recovered consciousness. He woke up groaning, feeling his head. He must have remembered very quickly what had happened and where he was, for he looked at Linus, cringing.

"It's just luck you're living," Linus said sharply. "You won't get another chance. I want the truth and nothing else. Do you think I give a damn about your life? Not for a minute. In fact, I won't mind at all if I have to kill you. Understand what I'm saying?"

"Sure — sure, I understand," Erb said a little thickly. "But there's some things I don't know. About your father — I don't know for certain."

"Drop it, Erb," Linus snapped. "Who in the hell are you trying to fool? My father's dead — buried — and you know it."

The man gulped. "I — that's what they say."

"They say — who are *they*?"

"I mean, that was the talk. That your father and Homer and Mike, too — that is —"

Linus leaned toward him. "How did it happen, Erb? I want to know — step by step."

The man shook his head. "I didn't see nothin' That is —"

Linus waved his gun. He said, "Erb, you're making a mistake. One more, and you're finished. I want to know what happened to my father, to Homer, and to Sam Bellows. I want to know how it happened. And you're going to tell me, or you're going to die."

The man took another deep breath. He seemed to have reached some decision in his own mind. He said, "Linus, I tell you this, if it's any help. That day Holloway came — and stayed — it was like this. They rode out to see us late one afternoon, early in the week. It was a Tuesday, I think."

"Who was with Holloway?"

"Just two — Kansas and Al Durfree. The others came later."

"All right, get back to the story. What happened that Tuesday?"

"They just seemed to ride in, friendly like. Your old man — Frank — invited them in for coffee. Homer rode in, just about then, so he went in the house, too."

"Mike Bellows?"

"No. He was out in the yard with me."

Linus could picture the scene, and it was as innocent a one as you could set up. Three men ride in on a friendly visit. They are invited for coffee — the most ordinary thing in the world. Another man, the son of the ranch owner, joins them. And then what happens?

"Go ahead, Erb," Linus said, and he knew he was tense. "I don't know what happened next — for sure," Erb said. "I was outside. I didn't go in. I didn't see the shooting — if there was any shooting. That is —"

"Damn it, if you didn't see anything, what did you hear?"

"There was some shooting, Linus. In the house. There was some yelling, too, but not any words I could hear clearly. Mike Bellows was close to the house. He rushed in. I would have charged in, too, but I had to get my gun. By the time I could, Sam Holloway met me on the porch. He was smiling and he said nothing was wrong. The shots I heard was target shooting from the back windows. He invited me to look and see, and I did. The parlor looked all right."

"Where were my father and Homer?"

"I asked about them. Sam said they were in the back bedroom, getting some papers. Then Sam said he had bought the ranch, and did I want to stay here and — and I reckon that's about all."

"You never saw my father again?"

"No."

"Or Homer, or Mike Bellows?"

"Sam said next morning that after the deal had been finished, Homer and Mike headed for the mountains, to get you. Frank took off for Wyoming 'cause his brother got hurt."

"You didn't see anyone leave?"

Erb shrugged. "I try to mind my own business. Always been like that."

"The way Carl McMullen had it, my father and Homer were around home for several days, but couldn't get into town."

"If they was around here, I didn't see 'em."

Linus, hunkering down to the ground, stirred his finger in the sand. He spoke slowly. "All right, Erb. Now let's go back a little. I can figure what happened in the house. There wasn't much shooting, was there?"

"Not much — only a few shots."

"Father and Homer probably didn't have a chance. They must have been shot before they could reach their guns, maybe even in the back. And Mike Bellows, charging in, didn't have a chance either. Three men in the house, waiting for him. I reckon it's just as well you stayed out."

"I would have," Erb said, "but my gun was in the bunkhouse."

Linus doubted that. More likely, Erb played safe — and then was given a chance to stay on the ranch. There was a good reason to give him such an opportunity. If he was still around it was a good indication that everything had been on the up and up.

"Let's talk about something else," Linus said. "A few minutes ago you said you'd heard my father, Homer and Mike had been buried."

Erb shifted uneasily. "I'm not supposed to hear such things."

"But you did. So where are the graves?"

"I don't know. Honest to God —"

"Where are the graves, Erb?"

"I — it'd be just a guess, that is —"

"Make your guess."

"If, I was to look, I'd look down on the river."

"It's a long river."

"I mean, just beyond the grove, a little north of the ranch. Next day after — after what happened, that Kansas and that Durfree was down to the grove outa sight. Sam Holloway rode there, too. Ain't much in that grove but trees, unless —"

"Unless three new graves."

Erb Wylie was scowling. Linus stared at him, then looked around. They had ridden south as far as the edge of the desert, and the character of the land here was different from the valley. The low swells of the meadows had disappeared, replaced by low ridges and rounded dunes, with here and there clumps of mesquite, cacti and thorny ocotilla. There was little grass.

Linus stirred his fingers in the sand. He said, "Erb, who's closest to Sam Holloway?"

"It would either be Kansas or Al Durfree."

"And of the others, which are cow hands?"

Erb sounded disgusted. "None of 'em. Not one. They're fancy gun-toters, an' that's all. They don't like to get dirty. They don't like to sweat."

"There's a woman and her daughter at the ranch."

"Yeah, a woman they call Maria, an' a girl, Rita. She's been the cause of two fights already. An' I know somethin' else you ought to know. It's about that Glory."

"What about her?"

"She ain't no sister of Sam's. She's just a fancy woman he picked up in El Paso from some highfalutin whorehouse. There's gonna be some killin' over her — an' she ain't worth it."

Linus nodded, but for a moment he was silent, weighing this new bit of information. This background on Glory was interesting, and there might be a way to use it. How, just now he wasn't sure.

"Who's causing the trouble over Glory?" he asked bluntly.

"Rupe Singer," Erb said. "An' you won't want to believe me, 'cause Rupe's old and ugly an' you wouldn't think she would look at him twice. Even a whore. But I'm givin' it to you gospel."

Linus rolled a cigarette. He lit it and in the flame of his match he caught a glimpse of Erb Wylie's face — thin, gaunt, worried. A part of what he had said might have been twisted in order to improve his own position, but through most of his story Linus had been able to sense the truth. He glanced around again. There wasn't much to see. A lumpy earth, dark gray, purple and black — a shadowy world — no lights from the cloud-shrouded sky. And through the darkness the movement of the wind, driving at them, picking up sounds and stinging bits of sand. Up to the north, a rain building up maybe.

Erb cleared his throat. "Linus, what you gonna do with me?"

"Take you in to see Carl McMullen. I want him to hear what you've said."

98

"Then can I get out — fast?"

"That's up to the sheriff. He might want to hold you for a time."

"No, Linus. I can't stay here — not even in jail — not now."

"Why not now?"

"'Cause I've said too much. 'Cause Sam Holloway will finish me. That's for sure. I wouldn't be safe even behind bars."

"Maybe we can work out something," Linus said.

His horse had drifted some with the wind, and now Linus got up and walked that way, to catch the horse, remove the hobble and start back. But suddenly there was no reason to return. Erb Wylie had disappeared — vanished in the darkness. In all probability, the moment Linus had started after his horse, Erb had moved, as quickly and silently as he could.

Linus jerked a look from one side to the other. He shouted, "Erb! Erb, get back here. Don't be a damned fool."

The man didn't answer.

Linus tried again. "Erb, where you going? You've got no horse, and down here in the desert nowhere to hide. Stay where you are, and Holloway's crowd will get you, for sure."

His answer came from the darkness to the left, off to the west. "I'll take my chances this way, Linus. I know what I'm doin'."

"Think about it again," Linus shouted. "If we go to town, Carl McMullen will see that you're safe. If he won't do it, I will."

"No thanks, Linus."

"Damn it, man. Use your head."

The man laughed — and from the sound he seemed farther away. He called, "So long, Linus. An' if you're smart, you better run faster'n me."

Linus shouted at the man again, but he didn't get another answer. He mounted his horse and rode to the west, but he didn't catch another glimpse of the man, and after a few minutes he realized that searching the darkness was foolish. He could wait until morning, and if a rain didn't catch them and wipe out Erb Wylie's footprints, in an hour or so he might find the man. But almost certainly, Holloway's crowd would be heading this way, soon as it got light — and it wouldn't be a smart thing to get caught.

Scowling, he thought about what to do, and finally decided to head back for town alone. Maybe Erb Wylie had known what he had been doing when he struck off through the darkness. If he was wrong, that was his own responsibility.

CHAPTER
EIGHT

Susan was crying. She wasn't crying loudly or hysterically, but she wouldn't stop. Sam Holloway, holding her in his arms, stirred restlessly. He wondered how long he ought to put up with it. After all, she had wanted what happened. He knew that too well. He had been in this same position before, with other women, and he could make a few judgments. Tonight, back here in the Aldrich barn, there had been no contest — unless it had been to see who could please the other the most — and the quickest. Susan hadn't fought for a minute. If anything, she had been the most aggressive.

He had spoken kindly, gently, imploringly, but now he tried a gruff and half-angry approach. "Damnit Susan, cut out the tears. You're a grown woman. Act like it."

"I — I just can't help it," Susan gulped. "What are we going to do about it?"

"About what?" Sam asked.

"About — what we did."

"It happens all the time to grown-up folks," Sam said realistically. "We're not the first folks who ever used a haystack in a barn. Makes a perty good bed, doesn't it?"

"But, Sam — what if we — what if I —"

"If you're worried about a kid, it might not happen. No use crying about a thing like that 'less you're sure."

"Sam —" Her voice had dropped to a whisper. "Sam, we could get married, couldn't we?"

He shook his head, "Susan, I wish we could, but we can't. I've already got a wife in Texas."

Her answer was a wail. "Oh, no, Sam! No!"

He was lying, but damnit, he didn't want to get married — at least like this, because he had to. If he ever did choose a wife he'd be careful, too. He wouldn't want one who cried like a baby. Instead, he'd take a woman with spirit, one who was on fire.

Through Susan's crying he heard another sound, the drumming of hoofbeats. At a guess, someone was hitting the road from town. The noises grew louder. He abruptly sat up, and pushed Susan aside. The rider had swung this way, was pulling up in the yard.

Susan suddenly clutched him tightly. Her whisper was shaky. "Who can that be? If anyone finds us —"

"Quit worrying," Sam growled. "Chances are that's Kansas, looking for me. Anyhow I told him where I might be."

"You didn't tell him about me!"

"Course not."

He fumbled in the hay, found his gun, checked it in the darkness, and then stood up. The rider in the yard had dropped to the ground, and was heading for the barn door. When he got there he spoke. "Sam — Sam, you in there?"

It was Kansas at the door. Sam recognized his voice. He said, "Yep, what is it?"

102

"Sorry I had to bother you," Kansas said. "Hope I didn't bust up anything."

Sam smiled. He nearly laughed. He said, "All right, Kansas, what is it?"

"Coleman got away."

"The hell you say."

"Fellow saw him cut out of town hours ago. From his direction, I figure he might have went to Pueblo Mesa."

"By God, that's it," Sam said, and this time he did laugh. He had a reason to laugh. If Linus Coleman had gone to the mesa, he had gone to see Susan — but Susan was here with him. He hadn't wasted any time either.

"Sure, he might have gone to the mesa," Kansas was saying. "But by this time he could have come back. Only he hasn't come back. Now what do you think that might mean? Where do you think Coleman might have gone *after* he reached the mesa?"

"Yep, why didn't he come back?" Sam nodded. "Nothing for him on the mesa. Kansas, what do you think? If you was in his shoes —"

"I'd take a look at the place where I used to live," Kansas said. "I'd try to grab Erb Wylie. You know, Erb is the kind who would gab."

"Yep, you might be right. Get my horse, Kansas. He's tied to the front fence. I'll be outside in just a minute."

"Don't rush it," Kansas drawled.

Sam fingered his gun. Susan hadn't made a sound while Kansas was at the door but now she was getting to her feet, and she was sniffling. Sam was aware of her, but he was still thinking of what Kansas had said. Of all his men, Kansas was the steadiest, the most thoughtful.

103

And he was blazing hell if he got in a fight. He never talked a great deal but when he did it usually was important. His guess about where Linus Coleman might have gone could have been wrong. But it would be no mistake to do something about Erb Wylie. Definitely, Erb Wylie was a danger point.

Susan spoke hesitantly. "Why are you worried about Linus?"

Sam shrugged. "I'm not, so don't think about him. Think about me."

"I will too much. Sam — what about us?"

"We'll work things out."

She came closer. Sam put his arm around her and kissed her. Her face was wet and her mouth was clinging and her body, abruptly, was too soft and fleshy. Damnit, after a good tumble in the hay, why did a woman always have to insist on pledges and promises? And those damned tears . . .

"Sam, when will I see you again?" she was asking.

"In a day or so," Sam said. "Just as soon as I can. Now don't worry, Susan. You can get in the house alone, can't you? You'd better go. It's after midnight. Pretty soon the folks will be back from the dance."

Her voice sounded flat. "I can get in the house."

"I hope your headache is better," Sam said, and he laughed again, reaching for some way to lighten the moment. The fiction that she had a headache had been her excuse to stay away from the dance.

"I'm all right," Susan said, but that flat sound was still in her voice.

104

It ran through Sam's head he ought to spend a little time petting her, making her feel better, but the hell with it. He had things to do. He said quickly, "Be seeing you again, Susan. It was mighty nice."

He swung away and went outside. Kansas was waiting in the yard, mounted, holding Sam's horse. Sam pulled into the saddle.

"We'll cut through town, pick up the other men and head for home," he said.

That took a little time, but not much, and soon they were riding up valley, Sam, Kansas, Al Durfree, Turk Kiley, Rupe Singer, Sim Ellsworth and Glory. Glory wouldn't hurry, so Rupe Singer dropped back to ride with her.

As the miles slipped past them, Sam tried not to worry about Linus Coleman — and actually he didn't. Tonight, or tomorrow, or the next day, they would catch up with Coleman. That was almost inevitable. And he would drop out of sight — just like his father and brother and a few others. It would be reported he had gone to Montana. And if necessary, Sam would have a friend in Montana write that he had met and talked to Linus Coleman. That should be enough to quiet all rumors. One more thing. If he got married to Susan, that would establish his position in the valley. It would make him look solid.

Al Durfree reined in closer and called, "Hey, look! Lights in the bunkhouse."

"Poker game, maybe," Sam said.

But he wasn't sure of that, and suddenly he was riding faster. They pulled up in the yard, and as they did, several men came out. The news they had wasn't good. Linus Coleman had been here, and had left an hour ago. He had kidnaped Erb Wylie. But more than that, he had shot and killed Art Deneen.

The clouds blew away some time during the night, and in the morning when Jean looked out, the sky was clear. The winds had stopped, too. It looked like a beautiful day.

Right after breakfast, she and her parents started for town, dressed for church. It should have been a nice drive, but strangely, it wasn't. Weller Talbot was glum and silent, lost in his own worries. Mrs. Talbot was worried, too. So was Jean. She was angry at herself for the way she had thrown herself at Linus. She was ashamed of the way Susan was acting. She was concerned over her father's attitude toward Sam Holloway. And she wished her mother had more gumption.

"Weller," her mother said, "are you sure Susan will be at the church?"

"Why not?" Talbot asked.

"It's just that — that the Aldriches aren't church people."

"Susan'll be there," Talbot said.

She was, but she didn't look well. Her color wasn't good, and Mrs. Talbot couldn't have failed to notice. She started, "Susan —"

"It's all right, mother," Susan said quickly. "I had a bad headache last night, but I feel better this morning."

"What gave you the headache?" Jean asked.

Susan smiled. "Something I ate. We better go into church."

106

Jean looked at her sister rather closely. Susan seldom complained of headaches and underlying her attitude this morning was a nervousness that was very apparent. Something more than a headache had made her shaky.

Linus Coleman wasn't at church, but Jean hadn't expected him. Sam Holloway wasn't there either — and that was unusual. Since he had come to the valley, he never missed a Sunday service. Jean frowned at her hands folded in her lap. What had happened last night — or this morning? What had Linus done, and did Sam Holloway's absence have anything to do with him? She bit her lips. She wasn't supposed to be worrying about Linus Coleman. That was Susan's department. And Susan, definitely, was worrying about something. Her face was so pale and drawn she looked almost old.

After the service they went outside, and there, surprisingly, she saw Linus and the sheriff, standing together, talking. Mr. McMullen was scowling and Linus seemed very grave. But he was alive — whatever had happened late last night or early this morning, he didn't look as though he had been hurt. Jean waved, instinctively, forgetting Susan was with her. And Linus waved and started toward her.

He walked toward her — and right past her, to speak to Susan. He said, "Susan, Susan, you don't know how I've missed you. I wish —"

Jean didn't hear any more. She walked away, quickly, to where their buggy was tied. And on the way she almost ran over the Barkweths. Her eyes had been too teary to see them.

As was usual on nice Sunday mornings after church, the people gathered around for a time, visiting and talking. Linus had drawn Susan to the side, and he seemed to be talking to her rather earnestly. Susan seemed to be objecting. She was shaking her head.

A man's voice interrupted Jean's observations. "Mornin', ma'am. Been waitin' to see you."

She swung toward the sound of the words and was startled to see Turk Kiley, the man who had run into her the day before. Big, ruddy-faced and grinning foolishly. Grinning, but not with his eyes. His eyes were dark and sharp, like a snake's.

He spoke again. "Ma'am — Jean — why don't I ride out to the mesa this afternoon? Maybe you an' me —"

"No thank you," Jean snapped.

The man laughed under his breath, but he seemed to be laughing at her. "No sense tryin' to dodge me, kid. I get what I want."

"Get away from me," Jean said. "If you don't —"

A sudden shiver seemed to grip her. It choked off her voice. Staring at Turk Kiley she realized that if he ever did get her away, off alone, the results might be disastrous. She could almost feel his brutality.

"Yep, I'll be out there," the man said. "I'll —" He broke off, stiffening, and looking over her shoulder.

Someone joined her — no, two people: Susan and Linus.

"Hello, girl," Linus said. "That a friend of yours?"

She shook her head. "No, I —"

She was suddenly afraid that Turk Kiley and Linus would have trouble, but nothing like that happened. Kiley twisted around and walked off.

Linus touched her arm. "Listen, girl, if that man has been bothering you —"

"He just stopped by, I suppose," Jean said. "I didn't ask him to. But I'll be all right."

"Isn't he one of Holloway's crowd?"

"Yes." She noticed Linus was watching Kiley rather curiously. She said, "You didn't — that is, you said —"

"Things worked out," Linus said. "Had a little trouble, but that couldn't be avoided. For the next few days I want you to stay close to the house. And, Susan, I'm going to see your father. Life isn't worth living if you have to live in fear."

Susan bit her lips. "I don't want you to bother my father. You don't understand him."

"I'll be over anyhow," Linus said, and he sounded angry.

Jean almost said he could come and see her any time, but she didn't. For the moment she had forgotten Turk Kiley. She looked narrowly at Susan, then at Linus, and made a quick guess that they had been fighting. But sadly enough, that might not mean a thing. You could fight with a person because you loved him.

"I'll be over," Linus said. And he seemed to include her in his promise. At least he smiled at her. Then he walked away.

Jean stared hard at her sister. "Well, Susan?"

"Well, what?" Susan answered.

"Is it to be Linus or Sam Holloway?"

"I may want both," Susan said, and she smiled.

It was a tight smile, a forbidding smile. Knowing her, Jean realized that for the present Susan was going to be difficult, superior and mysterious — and the truth wouldn't be in her.

CHAPTER
NINE

McMullen was talking to Henry Nugent, the banker. They were standing in the shade at the side of the church. Mrs. Nugent was in front of the doors, with some of the women, but she was beginning to throw anxious looks at her husband. Linus noticed that and as he passed her he called, "I'll break it up, Mrs. Nugent. Just give me a minute."

She waved and nodded. "Thanks, Linus." Then she added, "How's your father?"

"I haven't heard from him," Linus answered.

He walked on to join McMullen and Nugent, and McMullen said, "I've just been asking Henry about Sam Holloway's connections at the bank. Haven't learned much."

"I've told you as much as I can," Nugent said. "A bank is a confidential enterprise. How much money a man's got is his own business. Of course, if you had a court order —"

"We may want that later," Linus said.

"You know, I've been thinking," McMullen said. "Maybe we've learned something, after all. Henry says Sam Holloway hasn't opened an account. Said he was going to, soon as he got around to it, but he's put it off."

111

"What does he do about money, carry it with him?" Linus asked.

"No, Henry says that Holloway's left a strongbox at the bank. It's in the safe. Several times Holloway's gone to the bank to dip into it. If we could take a look inside —"

"You can," Henry Nugent said, "if you get a court order."

"We'll think about it," the sheriff said.

They talked for another minute, then Nugent turned away and rejoined his wife. Linus and McMullen drifted toward the street. A good part of the crowd was gone.

"Did you notice Turk Kiley here a few minutes ago?" McMullen asked. "Or maybe you don't know him."

"I don't know him," Linus said. "But I spotted him yesterday. I think he was bothering Jean Talbot."

"The hell he was."

"Didn't put up a fuss. Walked off the minute I showed up. Don't mean he was afraid. It was just —"

"Yep, I know what you mean. He didn't step out of line. None of Holloway's men ever do. I've got to admit one thing — Sam Holloway sure rules his own roost. If he and his men are bad as we figure, they do it under cover. Let's walk over by the livery stable."

"What's over there?"

"Just curious," McMullen said, and he smiled. "Got a number of friends who tell me things. Ziggy Meyers helps check folks in and out of town — folks I'm curious about. For instance, last night late, after midnight, Sam Holloway collected his men and they all took off

112

up valley. One was Turk Kiley. Just wonder when he got back. Might tell us nothing, or it might say a lot."

They walked on, Linus nodding. Then a thought crossed his mind and he said, "Where was Holloway last night, at the dance?"

"Was at first, but didn't stay. Not sure where he went. Rode out somewhere. Came back after midnight."

"You said Susan wasn't at the dance, but Ellie Aldrich was, and her folks, too. Susan was supposed to be staying there."

"You just talked to her. What did she say?"

"Nothing about last night. I didn't ask her."

McMullen shrugged, looked away. "Wouldn't worry if I was you."

Linus slowed down. He rolled a cigarette, lit it, taking this time to wonder why Susan hadn't gone to the dance, and to wonder if this had anything to do with Holloway's absence from town. Susan and Holloway could very easily have met somewhere. He didn't want to think about such a possibility, but he couldn't help it.

Susan had acted quite strangely this morning. She had been evasive. She said she didn't want him to come to see her, and had blamed it on her father's fear of Sam Holloway. But not too long ago when her father had ordered her not to go out at night she had slipped through the window to meet him by the springhouse. If she had wanted to, she could very easily have arranged to meet him tonight.

"I don't like it — Turk Kiley bothering Jean," McMullen growled.

"I don't either," Linus said.

He didn't add any more to that, but he shifted his thoughts to Jean. Now there was a girl you could understand. You knew instantly how she felt. She didn't hide her feelings. She stood up for what she believed. If she was just a little older — but damnit, she *was* older. Or at least she was no longer a child. If he wasn't careful, he would start getting ideas about her.

They reached the livery stable, turned into the yard and now walked toward Ziggy Meyers. He was just inside the open barn doors, out of the sun, and he was whittling. Ziggy, it was said, never stopped whittling except when asleep. He had done some nice wood figures. He was an aging man, wrinkled, bald and toothless, and he seemed to have no family. He had been in Orotown nearly ten years, but during that time, so far as was known, he had never said where he was from or what he had done. And ordinarily he didn't talk much. Linus was faintly surprised that Ziggy would say anything.

"Hi there, Ziggy," McMullen said. "Nice day."

"Maybe," Ziggy said. He looked from the sheriff to Linus, nodded to Linus, then returned to his whittling.

"Was just wondering," McMullen said. "Turk Kiley started up valley last night, but here he is in town again."

"Yep. Rode in early, afore sunup, with Kansas."

"So Kansas is here, too."

"Reckon he is. Figurin' time an' distance, them two men coulda just about made it to the ranch and back. Reckon they missed out on any shut-eye."

"Anyone else here from Holloway's?" the sheriff asked.

"None rid by here."

"Thanks, Ziggy."

The old man grunted. He eyed the figure he was whittling, then looked up abruptly at Linus. "What you up to, son?"

"Just digging into a few facts," Linus shrugged.

"Hell with facts. Know enough to put two and two together, an' that's plenty. If I was you, I'd act in a hurry. If you don't, you'll collect a bullet."

"Maybe I can duck," Linus said grinning.

They turned back down the street. Earlier, Linus had told McMullen what had happened at the Coleman ranch. He had explained what Erb Wylie had said and described how Erb had escaped. Now McMullen made a reference to Wylie. "Sure wish you'd kept your hands on him. Mighta helped."

"I doubt that," Linus answered. "He didn't actually confess a thing. He told me a few things that might help, but that's all."

"Still wish we had him," McMullen said. "Suppose Holloway rides in and accuses you of shooting Art Deneen."

"I might have to — disappear."

"Sure — ride out somewhere and meet a crowd of Holloway's men. How long would you last?"

"We've got to push Holloway into the open."

"Sure, but how?"

As they moved along the street, Kansas stepped into sight from the Round Corral saloon. A tall thin man, rusty-haired and freckled, pleasant-looking, still young. He fingered a cigar, stuck it in his mouth and lit it, glancing from side to side. He couldn't have helped noticing McMullen and Linus.

"That man's got the cut of a gunslinger," McMullen growled. "Watch 'im."

"I think I'm still being left alone," Linus said. "But one of these days . . ."

As they drew nearer, Linus waved casually.

"Nice day," Kansas said, and he seemed half amused at something. Then he surprised them. "What did you do with Erb Wylie? Finish him?"

Linus stiffened, not sure what was ahead. He was glad he was wearing his holster gun under his coat. How fast he could get to it he wasn't sure, but if it came to that —

"Don't get all stirred up," Kansas was saying, and he seemed to be enjoying himself. "Sam has told us to leave you alone, but I ain't sure he'll keep on sayin' that. An' killin' Art Deneen was plumb foolish. Rupe Singer thought a lot of Art."

"How do you feel?" Linus asked.

"Me? I look after myself first. If I got to I stomp on somebody's neck. Might be you're in line."

"Let me know if that happens."

"I'll let you know. Now what about Erb?"

"He got away."

"You don't say."

"He got away — after he talked some."

Kansas shook his head. "That's what I was afraid of. Course, what he said ain't gonna help you any. Erb didn't know too much."

"He told me several things."

"That so? You gonna get me arrested?"

116

McMullen leaned forward. "Step outa line just half an inch and you'll get packed in jail so quick you'll be dizzy."

"Nope, I'll never see the inside of a jail," Kansas said. "That's a promise I made to myself. You two men ever do any thinkin'?"

"Maybe you do?" Linus said.

"Yep. It sometimes helps," Kansas said. "Now about this Rhymer Valley. Sam Holloway has got himself pretty well set in. Folks like him. No reason why everyone shouldn't get along. That way, we'll all be happy. Most of us, I mean. But on the other hand, maybe you want to stir up a fuss. Do that and you'll be sorry. Sam can turn sour and mean — mean as hell."

"I can turn mean myself," McMullen said.

"Point is, you ain't got a chance," Kansas said. "Too bad, but that's the way things are. If I was you, I'd think about it. Now I gotta be goin'."

He grinned and waved, and both grin and wave were insolent, mocking. Turning away he slouched across the street. From the saloon door he shouted for Turk Kiley. After a moment Kiley appeared, and the two men headed for their horses.

Watching them, Linus said, "Mac, what do you make of it?"

"I'm so mad I could choke," McMullen growled. "The nerve of the guy — made me feel like I was crawling."

"But why would he open up like that?"

"He didn't tell us nothing we don't know."

117

"That's true enough, but why would he have said what he did?"

McMullen was silent for a moment, and then said, "Linus, I'm not sure, but maybe this kind of talk pushes us closer to an open break. It's like daring us to start something. It's like rubbing salt in a wound. I suppose we should flare up and do something reckless — and I'd like to."

"I've felt that way since the day I got back," Linus said.

"You got more patience than me."

"No — you've been standing back, but keeping your eyes open. And that's the way you've got to continue — slow and easy as far as we can, back water until everything's clear — if we can."

"We ain't gonna get the chance to lay back," McMullen predicted. "If Holloway is half as smart as I think he is, he'll start pushing us. Right now, there's just you and me who know what's been happening. Holloway's got a small army."

That was true. Holloway couldn't afford to temporize too long. He needed to smother the rumor which might hurt him, and the presence of a Coleman in the valley, asking questions, was just too much.

"Time to get home for dinner," McMullen said. "Fried chicken."

He had brightened up, and Linus had to laugh. One thing you could almost be certain of with regard to Carl McMullen. He never missed a meal if he could help it.

★ ★ ★

McMullen's guess, that Holloway would start pushing them, proved to be true before the next two hours were over. At the sheriff's home, and just after dinner, they heard horses outside, and Ken, moving to the window, called, "Dad, it's Sam Holloway — and several men with him. They're pulling up in front."

"I'll see 'em outside," McMullen said quickly, and he got up from the table, took a final sip of his coffee, then added, "Ken, you stay here with your mother. You too, Linus. I want you out of sight until we know what this is about."

"I'll be just inside the door, in case I'm needed," Linus said.

The sheriff crossed to where his gun belt was hanging. He put it on, checked his holster gun, and stepped out on the porch. He called, "Hello, Sam."

The door stood slightly ajar. Linus could hear what was being said outside, and through the lace curtain of the door's window he could see what was happening. Accompanying Sam Holloway were Kansas and Turk Kiley, who must have met their boss on the road. And three more were with them, Al Durfree, Rupe Singer and a fellow he didn't know by name.

"Hello, Sheriff," Sam nodded. "Hate to bother you at home and on Sunday, but this is rather important."

"I'm used to things like that," McMullen said.

Sam pushed back his hat. "Know where Linus Coleman is? I suppose he's around town somewhere?"

"Could be."

"Might even be in your house, huh?"

McMullen dodged that question. "What's this all about, Sam? Let's have it straight."

"All right, I'll give it to you straight, but I want to say this first. I'm sorry as hell about what's happened. I don't like violence. I don't —"

McMullen gestured with his arm. "You're starting a speech, Sam. Save it for someone who might believe it. Get to the point."

"Sure, I'll get to the point," Sam said, and his voice sharpened. "I want Linus Coleman arrested. I want him thrown in jail."

If McMullen was surprised it didn't show. "Maybe you got a reason."

"Two reasons," Sam said. "No, by God, three. Last night Linus Coleman busted into the bunkhouse at home. He killed one of my riders, Art Deneen — killed him as he was layin' in his bunk. He kidnaped another man — Erb Wylie — rode him to the river and hung him. We found his body this morning."

"Anything more?" McMullen asked.

"Anything more!" Sam cried, and he leaned forward. "Anything more! My God! What kind of sheriff are you?"

"Figure I'm a good sheriff," McMullen said. "Got elected, then re-elected six times. You ever run for office?"

"To hell with your record," Sam answered, and he was still shouting. "What I want to know is this: What you gonna do about Linus Coleman?"

"Figure to do what I should," McMullen said.

120

"An' what does that mean? By God, if you're not going to throw Coleman in jail, I'll do it myself. Or I'll send my men to do it."

"Do that," McMullen said, "and you'll find yourself in a peck of trouble. Long as I'm sheriff, I'm sheriff, and that's that. You or your men start after Linus Coleman, and you'll end up in jail yourselves."

"So that's it, huh? Ain't gonna do nothing about arresting Coleman."

"Didn't say one way or the other."

"You don't have to. Coleman's a friend of yours."

"Matter of fact, he is. But that don't cut no ice."

"The hell it doesn't," Sam said. "I can see just what's ahead. You won't do a thing. Sorta leaves it up to me."

"Nope. Like I said —"

McMullen didn't get to finish. Sam raised one arm, gesturing to his men. He cried, "The hell with it. Come on, fellows. Looks like we got a chore on our hands."

He wheeled away. The others followed. Most, Linus noticed, were scowling and seemed on edge. But not Kansas, who seemed amused, as though he had expected something like this.

McMullen came back inside. He looked quickly at his wife and said, "Now don't you worry. Things'll work out."

"I always worry," Mrs. McMullen said. "It's like a pain in the side that won't go away. I go on in spite of it."

The sheriff made an angry motion with his arm. "They had no right to come here, almost busting into the house."

"They didn't bust into anything," Ken said. "Dad, you were great. I was proud of you."

"So was I," Linus said. "I think Sam Holloway expected to walk right over you. He didn't."

"But what'll he do now? I tell you this — he's not going to take over my badge. I'm still sheriff."

"He knows it." Linus said.

"But that might not stop him."

Ken had stepped to the window. He called, "Dad, they haven't gone — or at least they haven't gone far."

"That so?" McMullen said, and he walked to the window.

Linus followed him. He peered down the side street in the direction of the main part of the town. Not far from the sheriff's house, Holloway and his crowd had stopped, and seemed to be in a conference. Then Holloway pointed, almost in a circle, and his men spread out. In a few more minutes Linus could understand Sam Holloway's temporary plan. From half a dozen points, Holloway's men surrounded the house, and right now that was all they were doing — watching.

But McMullen didn't like it at all. He swore under his breath, clenched his fists, and the corded muscles in his arms bulged in hard lumps. "Penned in my own house," he grated. "What kind of a man am I? I ought to bust out there and cut a few men down."

"No, not that way," Linus said. "We're getting sand in our eyes. Suppose we get it out."

"How?"

"Figure the smart thing to do," Linus said. "When the enemy is bigger than you, you've got to use your head."

122

The older man took a deep breath. He nodded almost wearily. "I know, Linus. But damnit, let me spill some of what I feel."

"I could leave," Ken said. "They wouldn't bother me. I could get to Hoke Kenney, Judge Greer and some of the others in town."

Linus shook his head. "No. We don't want an open fight — not yet. Suppose we sit out the afternoon."

"Then what?"

"I don't think Sam will do a thing — if we just wait. Sam wants to be popular, well liked, respected. And you can't earn those things by attacking the sheriff's home, or by putting on a shoot-out right here in town. Sam's doing two things — bluffing and trying to get you mad enough to do something wrong."

"What happens if we wait?"

"Who knows, Mac? Sam might pull his men back, or they might keep watching. If we can stall until dark, I've got a chance to get away."

"Away — where?"

"Several things we can try. One is the grove where maybe we'll find some graves — the grove near our ranch — the one Erb Wylie mentioned. If we had something definite on Sam Holloway —"

"I'm gonna walk out there an' see what happens," McMullen said.

He did, and nothing happened. He walked toward one of Holloway's men, faced him, talked to him and then returned. He still looked angry.

"Well?" Linus asked.

"That man I talked to — Turk Kiley — just said he was waiting for a friend and he asked what was wrong with that. The hell with 'em."

"Suppose we just wait and see," Linus said.

An hour passed, then another. Sam Holloway had changed his plan. He had pulled his men back so it couldn't be noticed they were watching the sheriff's home, but he managed the same thing by keeping one of his men riding by, circling the house. And he shifted men so that what he was doing wouldn't be too apparent. They seemed fairly sure Linus was in the sheriff's home.

McMullen calmed down after a while. He still didn't like being watched, but he seemed to be getting curious about Holloway's next step. Maintaining a guard after dark would be quite a difficult matter.

Ken, still excited by the possibilities of trouble, spied from the window, and kept track of the men watching the house. His mother tried to get him back to his studies, but he stalled her off.

Linus napped. He hadn't meant to, but he hadn't had any sleep the night before, and he stretched out on the couch, and without realizing it, fell asleep.

It was late in the afternoon when he awoke, and at first his mind was foggy, and he was muscle-tired as though the nap hadn't helped. He felt grumpy, too, and could feel a scowl on his face. Mrs. McMullen brought him some coffee and it probably was good coffee, but it tasted bitter.

When he could remember what had happened, and as his thoughts started working, he noticed McMullen

124

in his chair, chewing his pipe, looking glum, and Ken still at the window. He spoke to the boy. "Those men still riding by?"

"Riding by or watching from a distance — watching from different points. You know, this man Holloway is clever."

"Sure, he's clever," Linus conceded.

"He's kept a watch on the house all afternoon, but I doubt if anyone in town has noticed. Almost any time one of us could go outside, and maybe not be seen. But if we'd tried to walk away, or ride away, we couldn't have gone far without Holloway finding out."

"Sun must be about down," Linus said.

"It's back of some clouds, but low. It'll be getting dark pretty soon."

"And then what?"

"If they intend to guard the house, they'll have to get closer. And it will take quite a few men to do the job."

Linus ran his fingers through his hair. He knew he couldn't stay here much longer. He could say Holloway didn't want to stir up a fight, but he couldn't be sure of it. It might be that Holloway was desperate enough to risk anything, and after dark his men might try to bust in. If that happened and if there was any shooting, Mrs. McMullen or Ken might get hurt and this wasn't their responsibility. That meant he had to get out, and in the process let Holloway realize he had escaped.

"Soon as it's dark, I'll be leaving," he said slowly, "I'll grab a horse somewhere — maybe on the street — take one of Holloway's horses. Or I'll slip into the livery stable and get one from Ziggy."

McMullen stirred. "If you're heading for the grove near your place, I want to go with you."

"Then you'll have to get away from Holloway."

"I'll get away from him."

"Then, when you leave town, head for the mesa. I'll pick you up somewhere along the road."

McMullen got up. He walked to the door, looked out, muttered under his breath, and then went to the kitchen. Linus watched him and through the open doorway to the kitchen he saw McMullen reach into a cabinet. From a top shelf he took down a bottle of whiskey. He poured half a glass, started to drink it, but then stopped and shook his head. He set the glass down, covered it with a saucer and put the bottle away.

When he returned to the front room he mentioned the whiskey. "Figured it was time for a drink, and it is. But maybe we better put it off until later. Who knows what's ahead."

"You stay here until I'm gone," Linus said. "And if I were you, I'd duck another meeting with Holloway. By tomorrow, we might have some ammunition."

"I'm not the kind to dodge anyone," McMullen growled.

It was getting darker all the time. Linus glanced to the windows, then stood up. He said, "Almost time to go."

"Let me fix you something to eat," Mrs. McMullen said.

"Just a sandwich," Linus said.

He walked to the kitchen, and waited as Mrs. McMullen fixed him a sandwich, poured a glass of milk, and then set out a piece of cake.

"This has turned out to be a meal," Linus said, smiling.

126

"You could eat more, I know," Mrs. McMullen said.

Her husband came in, noticed the food and said, "How about me, Mom? Don't I deserve anything?"

"You eat too much, Carl," the woman said. But she started making him a sandwich.

From the front room, Ken spoke abruptly, and he sounded excited. "Hey, Dad, they've moved —"

Linus heard the crack of a rifle, and the sound seemed to come from in front of the house. He heard something else, too — a choking noise, a half-smothered cry.

He jerked to his feet, swung toward the front room, but McMullen was ahead of him. Above the man's shoulder he caught a glimpse of Ken, staggering backward. He seemed to be clutching his chest, and before McMullen could reach him, the boy lost his balance. He fell to the floor, turned on his side, a gush of blood streaming from his mouth. And the front of his white shirt was blood-stained. In a glance, Linus realized he was dying — or dead.

McMullen reached the boy's side. He dropped on his knees and the cry of anguish he gave made Linus shiver. His throat thickened, too, so he could hardly breath. He shook his head, not wanting to believe what he could see. He heard himself saying, "No, not Ken — not Ken. That bullet was meant for me."

But McMullen didn't seem to hear him. Linus looked around. Ken's mother had stepped into the parlor, and stopped abruptly. She had raised her hands to her throat and seemed to be trying to hold back the scream she was feeling. Her face, pale under normal

127

circumstances, had turned ashen, and in her eyes was stamped the horror of what had happened.

"He must have walked to the door, for some reason or other," Linus said. "Then someone outside —"

He bit his lips and was silent. There was no point in saying anything. He looked away, unable to watch McMullen and his son, unable to stand the expression on the woman's face.

McMullen got up slowly, releasing the boy, leaving him on the floor. On his wrists and hands and on the front of his shirt were blood stains from Ken's wound. But he seemed unaware of them. And he didn't seem to know anyone else was around, as he walked to the side of the room and reached up to the gun rack. He lifted down a rifle, made sure it was loaded and started for the door.

"Mac," Linus cried hoarsely. "Mac — wait a minute. If you walk out like that you'll get shot."

"Ken's dead," McMullan said. "I just want one thing — a chance at Holloway."

"You walk out there, and you'll never get it," Linus said flatly.

"The hell I won't."

Linus stepped toward him. "Mac — listen to me. This isn't the way —"

"I know what I'm doing."

He twisted away, turned toward the door, and Linus knew that argument was useless. He drew his own gun, stepped up behind McMullen, and used his gun barrel over the sheriff's head. The blow was hard enough to drop the man to the floor, and leave him momentarily unconscious.

Mrs. McMullen didn't seem to notice what they were doing. She had moved forward to kneel at Ken's side, and she reached out with one hand to touch his cheek. His eyes were wide-open, glazed. He couldn't have seen his mother but still she spoke. "Ken — Ken — it's mother."

Linus walked to her and touched her shoulder. "Would you like me to carry him to the bedroom?"

"Yes, Linus," the woman said, and she stood up. Thin, little, aging, tired, but still erect as she faced him. "He's dead, isn't he?"

Linus nodded.

"Things — happen," the woman said. "I would like you to carry Ken to the bedroom, then look after Carl. He will need you. Don't let him — I don't want to lose my husband, too."

Linus carried the boy to his bedroom, left him there with Mrs. McMullen, and returned to the parlor. McMullen was still unconscious on the floor, but he had started groaning and was showing signs of waking up. Linus walked past him to the door. It was partly ajar. He looked into the yard, but couldn't see anyone.

"Hey, out there," he shouted. "Thought you might like to know who was at the door a few minutes ago. It was Ken McMullen, the sheriff's son. You killed him."

No one answered. Maybe Holloway's men were nearby and heard him. Or they might have gone. Linus returned to McMullen's side, and waited for him to wake up.

CHAPTER
TEN

In the next half-hour, no one came to the door. As it grew dark, Linus locked the doors and windows. They hadn't turned on any of the lamps except in Ken's room, but the windows there had been curtained.

McMullen had been in the boy's room with his wife, but after a time he returned to the parlor, and he probably didn't see Linus in the darkness, for he called, "Hey, you still here?"

"Over by the front window," Linus said.

"See anyone?"

"No."

"Want a drink?"

"No."

"Damnit, I do," McMullen said. "But maybe I better skip it again — for a while. Need a clear head, an' what you done to it didn't help."

"I'm sorry about that, Mac. I tried not to hit hard."

"That's all right. It's good you stopped me. For a few minutes I was crazy. I still might go crazy if I ran into Sam Holloway."

"I know a little about how you feel," Linus said. "Of course, you got it all at once. It was a slower thing as I came to realize what happened to my father and to

Homer. But they're still dead, Mac. As dead as your son."

"We ain't doing anything."

"Before this happened we talked about going to the grove, up valley."

"Think we still have to? Seems to me what happened to Ken is proof —"

"We didn't see your son get killed. We don't know who fired the shot."

"We know who was responsible — Sam Holloway."

Linus shook his head. "No, we don't even know that. We can be pretty sure of it, but we can't prove it. Mac, we've got to get some solid facts, strong enough to stand up in court. Hell, you ought to know that. You've been sheriff long enough."

The older man sighed. "I'd like to forget that for a time. I'd like to act the way a father should after his son just got killed."

"You may get the chance," Linus said. "But in the meantime, how about the trip up valley?"

"I'd have to do a few things first. Get someone to stay here so Mom won't be alone. And I ought to see about the funeral, see Glover about doing what's necessary."

"Then do it. I'll wait here until you're back.

"No. Mom'll do all right. You better slip out the back, any time you can. I'll meet you on the mesa road in about an hour."

"In about an hour," Linus agreed.

He waited until McMullen left the house, then looked into Ken's room. He had meant to say something to the boy's mother, but he found her on her knees at the side of the bed, and he didn't disturb her. He walked back to the kitchen, unlocked the rear door and slipped outside. The next fifteen minutes he spent in working himself to the barn, and round to the rear, but he caught no sign of anyone watching the house.

Circling toward the main part of town where he might be able to pick up a horse, he realized abruptly he was near Katie's. Had it really been only last night that he had talked to her? So much had happened. So much that was ugly. In fact, the only pleasant thing he could think of from the past few days was Jean Talbot. And that was all wrong — he was in love with Susan. Or was he? That Jean —

Remembering her, Linus nearly smiled. And he took a moment to think about her, and to chuckle over the way he had grabbed her and kissed her last night, unaware that she wasn't Susan. That Jean — she had been almost without shame.

He stiffened suddenly, aware of a dark figure moving toward him. But the man turned aside, angling toward the rear door to Katie's establishment, and after a brief hesitation, Linus walked that way. Katie had been rather decent to him the night before. She had offered to help. She might already have some news for him.

One of the girls answered his knock, and led him to the parlor, but when she saw him she took a quick, deep breath and stepped back. Her voice was almost whispered. "You're — you're Linus Coleman."

She was tall, thin, rather young, brown-haired and pretty. Mac had described such a girl — Gail. Linus tried it. He said, "Hello, Gail."

The girl stepped quickly toward him, caught his arm. "You can't stay here. If they find out —"

"Who?"

"Kansas, Sim Ellsworth, Turk Kiley — any of them. If they find you here —"

"Then take me where I won't be found."

The girl bit her lips. "I can't take you to my room. He might come back. I mean Kansas. I expected him when I went to the door."

"Any empty rooms?"

"You can't stay here, anyhow."

"Why?"

"It's just — we can't have any trouble. If a house like this has trouble, they — they close it. We'd have to leave and that costs, and we don't make as much money as people think. So you just can't stay."

"Am I to be killed? Is that it?"

"I — I don't know."

"What did Kansas say?"

She shook her head. "I don't know. It's just — I don't want to talk about it."

"Are you afraid, Gail?"

She looked straight at him, then looked away. "Yes, I'm afraid — but it's not just Kansas. It's all of them. The ones I mentioned and the rest. Al Durfree, Bern Jorgensen, Fred Dustin, and that horrible Rupe Singer. They're like men I never met before. They're not human — they — I wouldn't stay here if it wasn't for

Katie. She's good. But these men — you'd better leave, Mr. Coleman."

The girl was frightened. There was no question of that. But she might know something of value, too. And she might be persuaded to talk. Linus tried a grin. He said, "Gail, think hard. Isn't there a room somewhere not being used — just a place we could talk."

She shook her head. "I don't want to talk. I don't even want to think."

"Where's Katie?"

"She's sick. This happens to her sometimes. She'll be all right tomorrow."

"Sam Holloway's never been here?"

"No."

"What about his sister — who isn't his sister?"

Her eyes widened. "How did you know about that?"

"Someone told me. What's her name, really?"

"Alice Gould. That's what they called her in El Paso. She worked at Myrtle's. If you've ever been to El Paso, you know it."

"Yes. So did several of the girls — and Katie, too. Katie's from El Paso."

"Has Alice been in to say hello?"

"In this business, you don't," Gail said. "But you've got to go, Mr. Coleman. You've just got to go. Any minute —"

As if on signal, someone knocked on the back door, and from a side room one of the girls appeared, on the way to answer the knock. She waved to Gail and Linus, but the parlor lights were low and she couldn't have seen them clearly.

134

"Well, where do I go?" Linus asked.

She took his arm and spoke quickly. "Up this way — but you can't stay. And I can't stay with you. If that is Kansas —"

She took him to one of the rooms but stood at the door, listening. The man at the door apparently didn't come in, but a minute later the girl who had answered the knock came back, searching for Gail. She gave her a whispered message, and Gail whirled around and said, "That was Paul Wertz, to warn us. Someone shot Ken McMullen. The sheriff's so cut up over it he can't do anything, so Sam Holloway is organizing a search. They think some stranger must have fired the shot. They'll be searching this house, just like every other place. If you're here —"

"Don't worry about that," Linus said. "I won't be here."

"There's another side door," Gail said. "It's hardly ever used. I'll take you there."

"Sure," Linus said. "Thanks."

He followed her, but his mind was working swiftly, analyzing what he had just learned. And it was so shocking it was hard to accept He had guessed Holloway was clever, but this latest step topped everything else. A few people in town might have noticed that Holloway's crowd had ridden to the sheriff's home. But they hadn't stayed, and although they had maintained a watch on McMullen's home, it probably hadn't been noticed. If McMullen accused Holloway of shooting Ken, the accusation would sound foolish. People might even think that the sheriff's grief

135

over the death of his son had affected his mind. So Sam Holloway, growing more popular all the time, was doing what any decent man should — organizing a posse to meet the emergency.

"Here we are," Gail whispered. "I wish — if you could have come some other way —"

"Might try it someday," Linus said. "Do you have room for another girl — Alice Gould?"

"That's not funny, Mr. Coleman. Alice has done what many of us have done — she's found a real position. I don't know why Mr. Holloway calls her his sister, but maybe —"

"Don't try to figure it out, Gail. And quit living in fear. It's not worth it."

She spoke bitterly. "Don't preach."

"Just think about it," Linus said. "Take the biggest mountain you can find, study it and study it, and most likely you can figure a way to climb to the other side."

"I'll get mountain boots," Gail said.

He grinned in the semidarkness and said, "That's it, Gail. Be seeing you."

He opened the door, slid outside and moved off through the darkness. Then, down the street, he borrowed a horse. It wore his father's brand. Right now, of course, the horse belonged to Holloway, or one of his men, but in a way he could claim it as his own. And he had no trouble in leaving town. If Sam Holloway's search was under way, it was operating in some other part of town.

Carl McMullen met him on the mesa road half an hour later. He asked, "Any trouble?"

136

"None at all," Linus said. "I stopped at Katie's on the way to pick up a horse."

"She have anything to say?"

"She was sick. I talked to Gail but I didn't get too far. She knew Glory, Sam Holloway's sister, as a girl in a parlor house in El Paso. Her name there was Alice Gould. Katie knew her, too."

McMullen shrugged. "Don't know how that can help us, but it's sort of interesting."

"Before you left town, did you do what you had to?"

"Talked to Mrs. Graham. She's going to stay with Mom, so she won't be alone. We'll have the funeral day after tomorrow. Talked to Glover about a coffin — and the grave. He'll talk to the preacher. I'll see him later. Mom will talk to him, too."

"You didn't see Holloway?"

"No, nor any of his men."

"I suppose I ought to tell you this," Linus said slowly. "While I was at Katie's a man came by with a message — Paul Wertz."

"He and Katie are old friends. It's one of those — situations."

"Anyhow, this was the message. Ken has been killed, maybe by some stranger. You're all upset, so Sam Holloway is organizing a posse to search the town, looking for the stranger."

McMullen reined up so sharply his horse reared into the air and then started bucking. It took a moment to bring him back into control, then the man looked at Linus. "If that's happening, why the hell are we here?"

"'Cause what we're doing is more important."

"But to let Holloway pull a stunt like this — my God, we're crazy."

"No, it's Holloway who's crazy — like a fox. Mac, right now he's laughing at us — and he can. If you rush back to town, and jump all over one of our best citizens, Sam Holloway, folks will look at you and say your mind has cracked."

"It's that bad?"

"Why not? We actually don't know who shot Ken. We don't know my folks are dead. Who is this Sam Holloway the folks are seeing? He's friendly. He goes to church. He doesn't gamble, or get drunk, or get in fights. He's nice to old women. Maybe if we get him mad — but we haven't managed it."

McMullen looked back toward town, then motioned vaguely with his arm. "The hell with it. You're right, of course. The search Holloway is making won't hurt anyone, but it'll build him up, and I don't like it a bit."

"Sure, he's getting big. That means that when he falls, he'll fall that much farther."

"Maybe."

"No maybe about it," Linus said. "Suppose we cut up valley while Holloway's busy in town."

Here and there up the valley were a number of stands of timber, and along the river from the break in the Blacks to below the town, trees marked the course of the water. A number of spots were called groves. Why some clumps of trees should have been called groves when others weren't, probably wasn't clear, but around the Coleman ranch what was called the north grove was a rather pretty spot along the river where they sometimes picnicked in the summer — and where Linus' mother had been buried. She had died long ago — so long ago Linus knew his memories of her weren't accurate. He attributed beauty to her, and a quietness and a gentleness — and the grove seemed to fit those qualities.

After a few miles up the valley, McMullen made a growling comment. "Erb Wylie could have lied about anything happening in the grove."

"Yes, he could," Linus admitted. "But he didn't sound as though he was lying, and I think he was planning — or hoping — to get away in the darkness. So maybe he told the truth."

"He sure didn't get away."

"No," Linus said. "He didn't."

Ken's death had so filled the time he hadn't had much opportunity to think about Erb Wylie and what had happened to him. It was easy, of course, to guess that Wylie had been caught — and early in the morning. His hiding place, then, couldn't have been very good. Or maybe he had tried to reach the stage road cutting through the desert, but hadn't had time. At any rate, Erb hadn't made his escape. He had been taken, probably questioned, then hanged, somewhere along the river. Galloway hadn't said where, but that might be interesting. And of course it had been a neat trick to say that Linus Coleman was responsible.

What they had called the north grove covered an area of about three acres and in parts of it the trees and shrubbery were so dense it didn't have to be searched.

But near the river and at other places there were clearings. A moon in the sky and bright, high stars gave a soft light to thin the shadows, but still under the trees and even in the clearings it was quite dark.

They tied their horses, then started pacing the clearings, and to Linus this was a grisly task — the hunting of a grave. Just thinking about it made his stomach churn. He wanted to find a place where the ground was soft, or where a mound didn't belong. He wanted to locate it, but at the same time he didn't.

It was Carl McMullen who discovered something. It was above the river and in a clearing fairly deep in the grove. He called to Linus. "Over here, I think. At least we could try."

He was testing the ground as Linus joined him. It was not a mound. What he had found was, rather, a depression in the ground, a spot where the grass was thin and new.

"Yes, we can try here," Linus said, and he suddenly felt shaky.

McMullen had brought a miner's shovel tied to his saddle. He went to get it, then started digging, working slowly and methodically.

"I ought to help you," Linus said, but he stood back, away from where the sheriff was working.

"That's all right," McMullen said. "Need the exercise. And anyhow, this keep me from thinking."

He went on working while Linus rolled a smoke. He still felt shaky inside, and his thoughts were completely confused. He didn't want the sheriff to find anything where he was digging, but at the same time he knew he

140

had to find out what had happened to his father and to Homer.

"Think I'm coming to something," McMullen said abruptly, and he paused for a moment to wipe his forehead and to look around at Linus. He asked, "What's wrong with you?"

"Nothing," Linus said. "You think it's —"

"Don't know yet," McMullen said.

He went on working, more slowly now. Linus watched him, then turned away and walked down to the edge of the river. He thought of his father, and of Homer, and stared into the shadowy darkness.

McMullen joined him after a time. He said what Linus had expected. "At least, we've found what we were after."

"Father and Homer both?" Linus asked.

"Both," McMullen said. "Third man with 'em, too. Third man probably was Mike Bellows."

"How were they killed, Mac?"

"Shot, near as I can tell. If I had more light, I could be sure. Want to take a look?"

"No. Later on, maybe. You're sure of it?"

"Didn't make no mistake, if that's what you mean."

Linus took a deep breath. It struck him that it must have amused Kansas, and probably Sam Holloway, to have buried the bodies here, in this grove not far from the cairn marking the grave of another Coleman — Linus' mother.

"We've got blankets here," McMullen said. "One on my horse, one on the horse you borrowed. I've got a rope. I could take one of those bodies, wrap it in our blankets, rope it well, and then we could pack it on one of the horses. We can't take more than one, but we shouldn't just ride off and leave. In a few hours, Holloway could move the bodies."

Linus nodded. "I know, Mac. Which body will you —"

"Your father's," McMullen said. "I want to get him to town. I want folks to see him. Then we'll be ready to move against Sam Holloway. We'll have a case that'll stand up."

"And two bullets could end it," Linus said. "One at you — one at me. We've got to get from here to town, and we've got to set up a reception for Holloway."

"You mean, if Holloway finds out what we're up to —"

"That's it, Mac. We're still just two people. You know how late it is?"

"Not too late. If we rush things —"

"The road isn't far from here. I haven't heard anyone pass on the way home. At a guess, Holloway's still in town, keeping his fingers on things. If we ride into town with a body in a blanket, how long do you think we'll last?"

"You're too damned cautious."

"Maybe I am, but I don't want to miss. Or if I do get smashed, I want things set up so someone else finishes the job."

"We could try this," McMullen said after a moment's silence. "We could head for the mesa. For Talbot's. Closest place I can think of."

"Sure, but there are three women at Talbot's. If anything went wrong —"

"We've got to take a few chances," McMullen said. "Anyhow, we won't stay there. We'll keep on to town or we'll swing down valley, and pick up some men to buck Holloway. Talbot can drive his wagon to town, with your father's body in it."

"Talbot might not want to get mixed up in it."

"The hell with that. We'll make him. I'll get things fixed. You get the horses."

Linus nodded. He wished they didn't have to turn to Weller Talbot, or possibly involve his wife, or Susan and Jean. But maybe he was just being overcautious. And surely, Talbot could take a chance on driving his wagon to town.

He had a smoke while McMullen was busy at the graves. He still didn't want to look at what was there. To keep his mind off of it, he tried to look ahead. As soon as they could prove what had happened here, most of the men in town and those down the valley would line up against Holloway, demanding some explanations. And maybe, without any fight at all, Holloway would run. At any rate, once they broke this story into the open, Holloway would be finished. He could be fairly sure of that.

McMullen came to get one of the horses. "We're nearly ready to ride," he said.

Linus started to answer, but then he stiffened, and looked in the direction of the road. Clearly through the night air he could hear the drumming of hoofbeats. More than one horse. Two or perhaps three. The sounds came nearer, tracing the course of the road. But they didn't slow down and a moment later the sounds faded to the west.

"Maybe a couple of Holloway's men, checking at home," the sheriff guessed.

That was what Linus had figured. "We'll ford the river," he suggested. "Head straight for the mesa. Ought to make it before dawn. Then, if Talbot will help us —"

He looked ahead, nodding. Why was he worried about Talbot? Of course the man would help them.

CHAPTER
ELEVEN

Sam Holloway paced the floor of the back room in the Round Corral saloon. Kansas and Al Durfree sat at the table. Kansas leaned back, examining his fingers. He didn't look at all concerned. Durfree was scowling, and now and then he would take a drink.

"This is a hell of a mess — a hell of a mess," Sam said, and he stopped to glare at Kansas. "Why did you take a chance? Couldn't you see who you was shooting at?"

"Thought I knew who I was shootin' at," Kansas said. "He was hunchin' over, just inside the door. Was liftin' his rifle. Figured he was about to shoot me. Figured sure it was Linus Coleman. Reckon I was wrong."

"You can say that again. What the hell are we going to do now? How can we explain it? You realize who you shot? The sheriff's son."

Kansas shrugged. "Pay me off, and I'll streak for the hills. You can join the posse ridin' after me."

"By God, I just might do it."

"The money," Kansas said. "I'll let you off for a thousand. Ought to ask for several. The money and cattle we've picked up —"

145

Sam motioned angrily with his arm. "Shut up. Lemme think for a minute."

"It always was hard, separating you from your money," Kansas said drily. "Course you figure if I get killed, you'll save some. But I'm not gonna get killed."

"Shut up for a minute," Sam growled.

He took another circle around the room, his expression changing. An idea had occurred to him. Of course the sheriff wouldn't like it. He might even tear his hair and scream. But let him. That, really, would improve his position. He took a deep breath, and then laughed softly. His head was sure working. That he could turn a defeat into a victory was the measure of his stature as a man, and as a leader.

"It's like this," he said slowly. "It was dark when the kid was shot, so we'll start the rumor that some stranger killed him — some man who hated the sheriff. A thing like that sounds reasonable. Folks won't question."

"So I don't have to run," Kansas said, grinning.

"I'm not through," Sam said. "We'll say that the sheriff is all busted up over his son's death. And to help him, we'll rake up a posse to search the town, looking for the stranger who killed the sheriff's son."

"But I don't see why the search," Durfree said.

"To set up this plan, I got to go to the sheriff, don't I? So you'll go with me. And if Linus Coleman is hiding there, we'll get him. Or if he's left, we can fake a search for a stranger, but keep after Coleman. If we spot him, we'll drop him — and say it was an accident. More important than that, however, is the reputation we'll get. We'll be labeled as good folks, anxious to help the sheriff even if he doesn't want us. Now what do you think of that, Durfree?"

"Damned clever," Durfree said.

"How about you, Kansas?"

"Too clever. You know, Sam, time will come when you trip yourself over your own smartness."

"You just never see any farther than your nose, Kansas. Let's get things started."

Sam didn't think it was wise to set up a search with only his own men, and to enlist others and explain what had happened took time. So when things were ready and Sam, accompanied by several of his men, got to the sheriff's home, Carl McMullen was gone. They didn't find Linus Coleman there either.

Mrs. McMullen wasn't very pleasant with them, and Mrs. Graham who had come to stay with her seemed equally unfriendly. The sheriff's wife ordered them out of the house. And she wouldn't say where her husband was.

The search, which was continued for the next two hours, failed to turn up Linus Coleman. And about that time, learning that Sim Ellsworth's horse had disappeared, Sam figured Linus must have left town. That possibility gave him an interesting problem, and the sheriff was involved in it, too. Where had they gone and why — and what would they try? Linus had guessed fairly accurately what had happened in the upper valley. The sheriff probably agreed with him. But they had no proof — and couldn't get it — unless they dug in the right place. Even that didn't prove anything, completely.

After a time, Sam sent two men home, to warn those there to be on guard against any trouble. Then he made the proper speeches to Judge Greer and half a dozen other men in town. He attributed the sheriff's disappearance to his grief — or to the vague possibility that he was on the trail of the murderer of his son. He offered to continue helping any way he could. He was earnest, seemed concerned, and could sense he had improved his position in the community.

In the back room of the saloon, however, he let down a little, gulping a heavy slug of whiskey and spitting out some profanity. It was all very good to improve his position. And he had done a lot to undermine the reputation of Linus Coleman. But Linus was still at large and, wherever he was, he could still talk.

He had another worry, too: Sheriff McMullen. By this time, unquestionably, McMullen felt like Linus, and because of that he had to be listed as an enemy — and might have to be killed.

Sam had another drink, then he took a squinting look at Kansas. "Where do you think they are?"

"Don't know," Kansas said promptly. "Ain't worried about 'em. Don't know why you are."

"I'd just like to get this settled."

"So would I. When do these Chicago men get here?"

"Next month."

"That could be a hell of a long time."

Sam took another drink. It was unusual for him to drink so much in the early evening — or at any time.

148

Occasionally, he did go on a binge — like that time in El Paso when he picked up Glory. But most of the time he was cautious about the amount of whiskey he used.

"Yep, a hell of a long time," Kansas said.

"They'll be here," Sam said, and he thought about that, nodding with satisfaction. In another month, representatives from the Land and Cattle Development would be here to pick up the titles to the land and properties in the northern Rhymer Valley — at a damned good price. A good price to the Chicago company, because they would be getting the land very reasonably. But an even better price to him, because he hadn't had to put up much money. Twice before, when this Chicago group had wanted to pick up new land, he had done the rough work necessary to make the deal. It was safer than robbing a bank.

He had another sip of the whiskey, and shifted his thoughts to Susan. Next time, she might be better. Maybe in a real bed she'd be a different woman. Glory would do, of course, but her general attitude and that strange tie she had with Rupe Singer left him uneasy. In some way or other he had to send Glory packing.

But as for Susan — he dug into his pocket, pulled out his watch and noticed the time. But maybe tomorrow he could ride that way. It wasn't a bad plan, he decided. Maybe, next time he saw Susan he would see her in the light, get a good look at her.

"We gonna stay here in town?" Kansas asked. "'Cause if we are, there's a little gal over at Katie's —"

"Yes, I think we'll stay overnight," Sam said. "Might be a smart thing to keep our fingers on things, but

149

don't get tied up over at Katie's. Might have to ride any time. I'll take several rooms at the hotel."

"Then — I'll be around," Kansas said.

Sam scowled at him as he left. Damnit, he was never sure about Kansas. The man worked for him, but not from any sense of loyalty or dependency. He took orders, but only if they suited him, or didn't bother him too much. At any moment, Sam knew, the man might walk out on him. He'd demand some money, too, and hard as that might be, it would have to be supplied. Kansas was too good with his guns. You couldn't argue with him. Usually, of course, he and Kansas got along pretty well, and Kansas helped keep the others in line.

Sam took another drink, then concentrated his thinking on Linus Coleman and the sheriff. In some way or other, and as soon as possible, he had to do something about them. They could wreck a neatly organized plan — so to hell with 'em.

Just as on the previous evening, Jean woke up suddenly. She sat up, looked toward the window and listened, straining her ears to catch any foreign sounds. At first she heard nothing unusual. Susan stirred, turned on her side and muttered something unintelligible. Jean glanced at her, frowning. Susan hadn't told her anything about what happened Saturday night, but something must have. All afternoon and this evening Susan had acted strangely, absent-minded, even worried. She had gone to bed early and when Jean came to the room Susan had been crying in the bed. She had stopped quickly and had feigned sleep — but she hadn't gone to sleep for a long time.

It was much later now — much later than when Jean had heard sounds outside the window Saturday night. The oblong of the window showed a light gray sky. It must be near dawn. What had wakened her Jean couldn't imagine.

She turned back the covers, and crossed to the window. Just an instant before she had heard the muted sounds of voices drifting this way, maybe from the direction of the barn. She squinted in that direction, then caught her breath. A man had stepped away from the thicker shadow of the barn — a tall, thin man. He pulled off his hat and ran his fingers through his hair — a characteristic gesture. She caught her breath. That was Linus over near the barn.

She looked around. Susan still was asleep. She could wake her and maybe she should, for Linus belonged to her. And it was wrong what she was doing, but as fast as she could she stripped off her nightgown and slipped into a dress. Then, once more, she climbed through the window.

Linus had stepped back into the darker shadows, but as she approached he walked out to meet her. He laughed softly and said, "Too bad, Jean. It's so light I can see you. Now if it was darker —"

"Don't you wish it were?" Jean said.

"If you were older, girl —"

"I told you I was old enough," Jean said, and she was angry. "Must I wait for white hair?"

He shook his head. "Just don't rush things. I suppose Susan is in there asleep."

"You can wake her. But be careful. She's cross in the morning."

"What a sweet sister you are."

Jean shrugged. "I just told you the truth. I wake up fresh as a daisy."

"I promise you're going to get spanked some day."

She backed away. "Try it, Linus. Try —"

A man had come around the corner of the barn — short, thick-bodied, and who he was Jean had no idea. She broke off what she was saying and pointed.

Linus looked around. "That's Mac — Carl McMullen." He raised his voice. "All set, Mac. I put — the bundle in the wagon."

"Who's this — Susan?"

"No, I'm never lucky," Linus said. "This is Jean. Maybe you ought to wake her father. We ought to get on down valley soon as we can."

He swung toward the house. "I'll see who I can wake up."

Jean glanced at him, then looked at Linus. "What did you mean about a bundle?"

"I want to tell you something else first," Linus said, and his voice had sobered. "It is pretty bad."

She stepped closer. "What is it, Linus?"

"Ken McMullen is dead. He was shot late this afternoon, in his own home. One of Holloway's men is responsible, but we don't know which one."

He went on talking, and he seemed to be explaining what had happened, but Jean didn't pick up any of the details. In the face of the simple enormity of Ken's death, she could think of nothing else. She hadn't been

152

in love with him — not as she was with Linus. But she had felt close to him — like one of the family, a brother. And now he was dead. The shock of it left her numb.

Mr. McMullen had wakened someone in the house, probably her father. The lights were on inside. And in a little while, probably, Susan would be up.

"Hey, you better sit down somewhere," Linus said.

Jean shook her head. She stiffened and said, "I'll be all right, Linus. It's just — kind of a blow to hear a thing like that."

"This is a blow, too," Linus said. "Not so hard, but it was hard to me. That bundle I mentioned — the one in the wagon — is the blanket-wrapped body of my father."

Again she caught her breath. "Oh, no!"

"There were three bodies in the same grave," Linus said, and his voice sounded flat. "Homer's and Mike Bellows' "

"Where did —"

"In the north grove, all piled in together."

"You think Sam Holloway —"

"Who else could have ordered it? I talked to Erb Wylie. He told me how it happened, but he didn't see it. He guessed where the bodies could be found, and now Erb Wylie is dead. He was hanged yesterday morning. Holloway said I hanged him, but Erb got away from me. Someone else caught him — and hanged him."

Jean shuddered. "Linus, what's happening all around us?"

"It's pretty ugly, isn't it?"

"I think I'm frightened. I wasn't before. Not really even when I was struggling with Bern Jorgensen. But now —"

Linus reached out to touch her shoulder. He shook her lightly. "Hey, we can't have any of this. You're a strong person, Jean. You've got to stay strong. Now come on, Mac is motioning to us to head for the house."

Her mother and father were up when she and Linus entered the house. Her father was talking with the sheriff, and Linus joined them. Susan wasn't up, but she was out of bed. Jean walked to the door of their bedroom, and looked in. Susan was dressing. Undoubtedly, from what she could hear she had guessed who was present.

Of course, Linus walked to meet her when Susan left the bedroom. He took her in his arms and this time Susan didn't seem to hold back. Jean watched them, bit her lips and then stared away. For a moment she hated them both — herself, too. But after a moment of self-abasement, she remembered her suspicions of Susan, and her attitude stiffened. She didn't know, honestly, just how far Susan had gone with Sam Holloway, but at least *she* never would have let him touch her.

They had breakfast. It was an awkward meal, without much talk, and twice Jean's father got up and walked to the front door to look outside. It was dawn by now, and from the front door he could see miles toward the edge of the mesa. He didn't say out loud what he was

154

thinking, but Jean could guess. Weller Talbot was afraid someone was following Linus and Mr. McMullen.

Jean was embarrassed by her father. She knew she shouldn't have felt that way. Her father wasn't the same kind of person as Sam Holloway or Mr. McMullen — or even Linus. It had been a religion with him to abhor violence. That was the way he felt, and that was all there was to it. Her mother felt that way, too. But what about her? At least, in what she had said, she hated violence, too.

McMullen spoke suddenly. "Weller, can you do it for us — wagon that — that bundle to town?"

Weller Talbot scowled, cleared his throat, looked around the table. "You know how I feel about things like this. I don't wan't to get mixed up in —"

"You want to take a look in that wagon?" McMullen said harshly.

"No, I don't have to do that."

"Then what about Susan and Jean? Holloway's had his eyes on both. You gonna be able to buck Holloway on your own?"

"It ain't that," Talbot said. "It's just —"

Jean squirmed for him. She thought she knew how he felt. He wanted to do what Linus and Mr. McMullen were asking, but to do it would make him a part of the coming struggle.

"Well?" Mr. McMullen asked, and his voice had sharpened.

"Reckon I can do it," Talbot said. "Sometimes a man has to shut his eyes to things."

Right after breakfast, Linus and Mr. McMullen left, to head down the mesa and into the lower valley. Jean didn't get another chance to talk to Linus before the men left. But Susan got that chance. She kissed Linus good-bye. She did it very prettily.

Then, during the next few hours, Jean did her work around the house. Jean's mother hadn't been well, so Jean and Susan divided the heavy work. Actually, as it worked out, Jean did most of the work. For a dozen reasons, Susan found ways to escape doing things.

This morning, Jean didn't mind having to keep busy. It kept her from thinking about Linus and Susan. Definitely, as things were developing, Sam Holloway would be destroyed and then Linus and Susan would be married. Susan would make a charming wife. She would never lift a finger to do anything around the house, which should keep her pretty and desirable. And if anything had happened between her and Sam Holloway — why, she would just forget it.

Her father hadn't left for town. Jean knew he was stalling about it. She looked out once and saw him in the scant shade of the barn. Bruce was with him, but that was to be expected. Inside or out, while her father was home, his dog dodged his footsteps. Right now Bruce was nuzzling her father's leg and her father stooped to pat the dog's head.

Jean went on working, but it was only a few minutes later when she heard someone ride into the yard. She looked out again, and was startled. The man dismounting from his horse was Turk Kiley. She

156

recognized him instantly. He had bumped into her Saturday, and then Sunday after church he had said he meant to come out to see her. He was a big man, and he didn't look too clean. He hadn't shaved and under the edge of his hat his hair looked long and ragged.

Talbot and his dog appeared from the barn, and walked forward. Talbot was smiling. He said, "Hello, there. What can I do for you?"

Kiley wiped his hand over his face, and it hit Jean suddenly that the man was drunk — or at least had been drinking. His words were thick, too, as spoke. "You're Talbot, ain't you? Got a young daughter. Want to see her. Get her out here."

Talbot looked surprised. "What's all this? I don't understand —"

"Just get the girl out here."

He half-shouted the words, and even the dog Bruce seemed to sense something was wrong. A deep growl rumbled from his throat and he stepped in front of Talbot.

"Get that damned dog outa here," Kiley grated.

Talbot said, "Here, Bruce. Here!"

But for once Bruce didn't seem to hear Talbot's order. In a half-crouch, he stared up at Kiley, still growling.

"The hell with you then," Kiley shouted.

He drew his holster gun, aimed it deliberately at Bruce and fired. He fired again and then again. Bruce reared into the air at the first shot, lunging at the man. But he never reached him and after he hit the ground, he didn't get up again. Instead, he rolled over, half on his side, half on his back, and pawed the air, yelping.

157

Jean, still watching from the window, saw her father looking down at Bruce, a stunned, unbelieving expression on his face. Then he stepped forward and knelt down at the dog's side. But Bruce had stopped pawing the air and was no longer yelping. He lay motionless — dead.

Talbot looked up. "Why? Why did you do that?"

"I just don't like dogs," Kiley said. "Get up on your feet. Get your daughter out here. The young' un."

Talbot didn't say anything. He got up, walked toward the house and came inside. Jean turned toward him, not quite sure what he was going to say, but he didn't seem to notice her. Nor did he seem to see Susan or his wife, who had moved to the other front window. He walked to where his rifle was hanging, on two wall pegs. He lifted it down, examined it, pumped it once and swung back toward the door.

"No, Weller, no!" his wife called. "You can't —"

He didn't seem to hear her. He went outside. At the first explosion of the rifle, Kiley staggered back and fell to the ground. But there were two more shots from the rifle, and in the silence which followed Jean heard her father's mutter: "*Three shots for Bruce. Three at least.*"

Shaky, and with his face gray and haggard, Jean's father carried Turk Kiley's body into the barn. There he probably covered it with a blanket. Then he started saddling his horse.

"Where's he going?" Jean wondered aloud. "He's got to take the wagon to town. Linus and Mr. McMullen are depending on it."

"If you want to worry about anything," Susan said, "worry about Father. Look what you've done."

"And what have *I* done?" Jean asked sharply.

"You brought that man here, and he worked for Sam Holloway. When Sam finds out —"

Jean's eyes narrowed. "Just whose side are you on, anyhow? I thought it was Linus you were kissing this morning. Who were you kissing Saturday night — Sam Holloway?"

Susan straightened. "I certainly wasn't, but it's none of your business, anyhow."

"At least, you're getting in shape," Jean said. "A few more experiments and you can go to work for Katie."

"Why, you little — I ought to —"

Susan was glaring at her, her fists clenched. She stepped forward, but stopped. A year ago, Susan would have slapped her, but once, not long ago, she tried it, and found herself on her back, and getting the worst of it. Since then Susan had been more cautious.

"Girls," Mrs. Talbot said. "Girls, please don't. You used to be such good friends."

Weller Talbot came in, interrupting them. To Jean, he looked sick — actually sick. "I'm going over to the ruins," he said. "I'll bury Bruce there. He liked the place."

"But the wagon," Jean said. "It's got to be taken to town."

"That'll have to wait. I — the way I feel about Bruce, that comes first."

He swung away, went outside, and in the yard picked up the dog. Holding him in his arms, he climbed into the saddle and started away.

159

"This way he won't get back until late afternoon," Jean said, and she looked at Susan. "I can hitch the team if you want to drive to town."

"I intend to do no such thing," Susan said. "And if you're smart, you'll do nothing either."

Jean looked straight at her sister. "I'm beginning to find out which side you're on."

"I'm still on both," Susan said.

She laughed infuriatingly — or at least that was the effect it had on Jean. She went out and started saddling her horse. She could do that, at least. A little while later she left, without saying where she was going but she headed in the direction of Orotown.

"I'm going there, too," Jean told her mother. "I mean, I'm going to town. I'll drive the wagon."

"You think you should?" Mrs. Talbot said. "If there is any trouble —"

"Now don't worry about that," Jean said. "I'll just drive the wagon to town. I won't notice what's in it."

She hitched up the team, started for town, and it was several miles before she got to thinking about Susan, and what Susan might be doing in town. Maybe she wanted to be there when Linus arrived, or maybe she wanted to see Sam Holloway. If she went to see Sam, was there any chance she might say anything about the wagon — and what was in it?

She shook her head, and then spoke aloud. "Susan wouldn't do a thing like that."

She hoped, terribly, she was right.

CHAPTER
TWELVE

Half a dozen miles from the Talbot place, but still on the mesa, McMullen signaled a halt, and he and Linus reined up. "Time to rest the horses," McMullen said. "Want to think a minute, anyhow."

That was really the reason they had stopped. Linus was sure of it. There was something on the sheriff's mind. The worry that was bothering him was stamped on his face.

Linus waited until he had a cigarette going and the sheriff's pipe was burning, then he said, "All right, Mac. What is it?"

"Just been thinking about Ken — and Mom sitting home alone. I know what I gotta do, and Mom never stopped me from what I thought was my duty. I mean, she ain't fussing that I'm not home, but damnit, I ought to be home at a time like this."

"Sure you should," Linus said.

"I mean, it would help a little if I just stopped by for a minute or two. I mean, maybe there's things I ought to help decide — about the funeral, I mean. It's just —"

"We could stop by there," Linus said. "We might even be able to ride in and not attract attention. I wouldn't want to try it if we had a body with us. We might have been stopped, might never have got any farther. Empty-handed, we can risk it."

McMullen nodded. "I been thinking about it. If we rode in from the east along the trees flanking Crandall's, we could get almost to town afore anyone saw us. Or you could lay back, and in a couple hours I could join you. That's all I need — maybe an hour with Mom."

"Why don't we try it, Mac?"

"Like I said, you don't have to risk it. If I get away again, we can round up our posse and have 'em back in town by tomorrow morning."

"Sure. That's soon enough," Linus said.

"Then we'll angle more toward town."

"Sure."

They rode on again, slanting toward the edge of the mesa. From Linus' standpoint, he was ready to rush things. They were ready to challenge Holloway and the sooner they did, the better. But realistically, he couldn't think only of himself. He had to consider McMullen. The price he had already paid was too high. Now if he felt the need to see his wife, such a thing wasn't unreasonable.

No one was home at Crandall's. They might have gone to town, and they might return any time. Or it might be late before they came home.

"You go ahead," Linus suggested. "Just be careful what you do — and avoid Sam Holloway if you can. I'll borrow Crandall's barn, and find a place to doze. For two nights now, I haven't had much sleep."

McMullen nodded. "Good. I'll go ahead. And if I see the Crandalls I'll tell them they have a guest, so they won't be surprised to find you."

He rode off toward town, flanking the line of trees, and when he was well along the way, Linus turned to the barn. He unsaddled his horse, rubbed him down and then fed him, and left him in one of the stalls. After that, he tried the hay forked up in the far end of the barn. It made a comfortable place to rest. In fact, five minutes after he stretched out, he was sound asleep.

McMullen woke him, and as he sat up, groggy from the sleep, he had a sense that it was late in the afternoon. The streaks of sunlight slanting in through the open chinks, and coming from the west side of the barn, indicated he was right. As another sign, he was hungry.

"Everything all right, Mac?" he mumbled.

"No. Nothing's right," McMullen answered, and he swore half under his breath.

"Your wife —"

"Mom? She's fine. But I can tell you this. Sam Holloway's been damned busy. You would think more people would trust me, but Holloway's been putting out a line that I've collapsed, that I've gone crazy with grief, that I'm liable to do anything. He's set up a town committee to act in what he calls an emergency, but he's calling the shots himself, backed up by his own crowd. He's moved into the hotel, practically took it over."

"Did you see him?"

"No, but I've got more bad news. Talbot didn't bring in his wagon."

"I can go after it."

"Too late for that. Jean drove it in but as she got here, Kansas met her, took charge of her and of what was in the wagon."

Linus stood up. He was suddenly shaky. "Where is she?"

"I think they took her to the hotel. Didn't see what happened myself. Got this information from Ziggy Meyers. No reason he wouldn't have told me the truth."

"What would they have done to her?"

"Don't reckon they've hurt her."

Linus was still shaky. It was hard to picture what might have happened to Jean. Maybe she hadn't been harmed but Holloway and the men backing him were on the point of desperation.

He checked his gun. "Let's go."

"Where?" McMullen asked.

"To town, and to the hotel. Where else?"

"Wouldn't help Jean a bit if you rode in and got killed."

"We can't just wait."

"We've got to. I've still got a few friends in town. Give me two hours and I'll have some backing. It'll be dark by then, too. We can close in around the hotel. Linus, we've got to have help. We can't lick Holloway's crowd alone."

Linus nodded. He knew what McMullen was advising was necessary. But to wait two hours — how could he wait two hours? In his imagination he could see Jean driving the wagon, could see her being met by Kansas. He could — but there was something wrong here. Jean shouldn't have been driving the wagon, and more curiously, why had Kansas met her? How could he have known what was in the wagon?

He put that question to McMullen. "Why did Kansas meet the wagon?"

The sheriff looked straight at him. "Want me to guess? It isn't a pretty guess, but if you want it —"

"Go ahead."

"I got this from Ziggy, too. Susan rode into town well ahead of Joan. She stalled for a time, then she went to the hotel, maybe to see Holloway."

"I don't believe it," Linus snapped.

"You don't want to. You know what you ought to do — take another look at Susan. Not at how pretty she is. Look at what she's done. That night of the dance when Holloway and Susan were gone, they —"

"That's enough, Mac," Linus interrupted. "Drop it right there."

"Sure. Guess I better get started for town. You wait here."

Linus nodded, but said nothing. He wished he hadn't asked that last question of McMullen. What Susan had done the night of the dance was her own business. He didn't want to hear any gossip. And surely, whatever else was true, Susan wouldn't have turned completely against him. If she had gone to town and had gone to see Holloway, there must have been a good reason.

He rolled a smoke, watched McMullen leave, heading for town. Then, in a few minutes, he decided to follow. In some way or other he had to get to that hotel. It couldn't wait. Maybe Susan was in no danger. If

Holloway was interested in her, she was safe. But Jean was in a different category. If anyone had hurt her . . .

Linus saddled his horse and headed for town.

Talbot knew he had taken too much time to bury his dog. He became especially aware of this when he got home and learned both his daughters were gone. Susan had headed to town on her saddle horse. Jean had taken the wagon.

He hurried after them, annoyed that Jean had taken the wagon. But that, he knew, was like her. Jean had always been reckless, impetuous. Maybe, as she grew older, she would quiet down, but he wasn't sure of it.

When Talbot reached town he looked around for the wagon, but it wasn't on the street. He reined up, tied his horse and headed for the general store. Inside was Sol Drews.

"Afternoon, Sol," he nodded. "Seen my daughters?"

"Susan was in earlier," Sol answered. "Think she went to the hotel to see —"

"Holloway?"

"Sure, but it was all right," Sol said quickly. "They was over at the dining room. I mean —"

"I suppose Sam is still in town. I noticed some of his men on the hotel porch."

"Yes. I think he's still here."

"Seen Jean?"

Sol gulped. "I — that is, no, I mean —"

He was lying. Talbot was sure of that. But why? And a possible answer slashed across his mind. Jean had driven the wagon to town, and in the bed of the wagon

166

had been a body. He took a quick, deep breath, and hurried away.

"Hey, Weller," Sol shouted. "Where you going? Wait a minute."

Talbot didn't wait. Right now, neither Susan or Jean might be in trouble, but at least Susan had been with Sam Holloway, this noon at the hotel, and that had to be stopped. And if anyone was going to question Jean's action in driving the wagon to town, that had been his responsibility. The one to talk with about these matters was Sam Holloway. He might as well see him and get it over with.

He slanted across the street, directly toward the hotel, and if the men on the porch noticed him, and watched him sharply, he wasn't aware of it. He climbed the porch, walked to the door and went inside. He didn't speak to any of the men he passed. Two men followed him to the lobby, but for the moment he wasn't conscious of them.

The lobby was large, a waste to the hotel but a convenient waiting place for ranch women in town for the day — and a meeting place for men who didn't care for the saloons. In the years that were past when Susan and Jean had been little girls, their mother had entertained them here while their father had been busy somewhere around town. They had grown up accustomed to using this lobby whenever they needed a place to go in town, so it wasn't strange or wrong that they might have come here today.

But neither girl was in sight. Then Talbot remembered they could easily have gone to see some friend. And

167

anyhow, what he wanted first was a brief talk with Sam. A friendly talk, but a blunt and honest one. Surely Sam would realize he was too old for Susan. And as for what Jean had done, she was just a child.

The place seemed deserted. Talbot hesitated, half-turned back to the street, then stiffened and swung back to look down the corridor. The door to the first room had opened and a man seemed about to leave. A big man, heavy, thick-bodied — Sam Holloway. But above what he had been saying a woman was saying something, speaking through her tears. "No, Sam. No. You can't mean —"

"Cut it out, Susan," Sam answered. "One thing I can't stand is crying. Now, your sister's a different article. An' if I want —"

"Holloway!" Talbot shouted. "Holloway, what's my daughter doing in there?"

The man in the doorway twisted to look at him, and he suddenly laughed and said, "Talbot, I'm glad you're here. Maybe you can help me with Susan. Never did know how to handle a woman when she turned on the waterworks."

Talbot scarcely listened. He shouted, "Susan — Susan, come here!"

He expected her to obey him. He expected her to rush toward him, or she might come shamefaced and stumbling, but she would come. Only she didn't — or at least, she wasn't hurrying.

Sam looked back into the room, and he seemed amused. "Give her a little time to fix up," he suggested. "She's had a rough afternoon."

Again Talbot took a quick, deep breath. When he had started to leave a moment before he had noticed Kansas and another man had followed him into the lobby. They were behind him now. He remembered that vaguely, but not as though they were important. The only one who concerned him was Sam Holloway, and now he could look at him with honesty. He had seemed genial, friendly, pleasant, but his was a lying face — an ugly face, vicious, filled with sin.

Very deliberately, Talbot reached into his pocket. He drew out his Colt, raised it and said, "Holloway, I'm going to kill you. I'm going —"

Something hit him squarely in the back. The blow took away his breath and it filmed his eyes so he couldn't see. In his ears he heard the blast of a shot, then a humming and a ringing. And a pain — a widening, blossoming pain which seemed to be enveloping him. But it happened fast. He had no consciousness of falling to the floor.

Sam watched him spill to the floor, and he glanced at Kansas, who was putting away his gun. He made a gruff complaint. "Why didn't you get closer so you could have slugged him? Now we got another problem on our hands."

"Maybe I shoulda let him shoot you," Kansas drawled.

"Nope, but you better get outside," Sam said. "Keep anyone from coming in. Say the shot was nothing — an accident."

Susan flew past him, hurrying now. She stumbled to her knees at her father's side, then looked up. Her eyes were glassy, shocked. "He's — he's dead," she whispered. "My father's dead."

A convulsion seemed to shake her. She bowed over, then straightened, and she stiffened. A scream started in her throat. Sam rushed toward her, but he wasn't quick enough to stop it — or at least to stop it completely. Susan started her scream and Sam broke it off with three or four hard slaps across the face. Then he hauled Susan to her feet and half-carried her back to the room.

She collapsed on the bed and lay there sobbing. Sam let her cry. Her crying wasn't loud. It was more like whimpering. He stood watching her. He couldn't see her face, but he knew it was pink and swollen from her crying, red-eyed, and not at all pretty.

To be honest, Susan was too fleshy, too puffy in the legs and arms and over the stomach. Maybe she had good breasts, but that wasn't everything. Jean probably had no breasts at all, but he had had a tussle with her and her body was muscled, warm and firm. Come evening and if he could calm things down he'd find out. One of the other men could have Susan. It would have to work out that way. He couldn't let either girl go. They knew too much.

Kansas showed up at the door. "Durfree's got things under control out on the porch. Someone asked about the shot and Durfree said it was an accident. That satisfied 'em. What about Talbot's body?"

"Put him in the back room — with the one that was in the wagon."

"We can hide that one, carry it out. But folks saw Talbot enter the hotel."

"We'll say he left by the back door after dark. So he rides away, and in a couple days it turns up he disappeared. By then maybe we can blame Linus Coleman."

"Sure — maybe," Kansas said. "I don't like the way things are lining up."

"Want to pull out?"

"Might."

"Then go ahead — and the hell with you."

"What you gonna do with the girls — Susan an' Jean?"

Sam lowered his voice. He glanced at Susan. She was still sobbing, but maybe she was listening.

"I know," Kansas said drily. "One of 'em you had. The other you want. An' you got Glory, too. Did anyone ever tell you you was rotton all through?"

"By God, you go too far," Sam half-shouted. "Get outa here."

"I'm thinkin' about it," Kansas said. He backed away characteristically, not turning until he was out of sight.

But Sam wouldn't have reached for his gun anyhow. Kansas might leave, but he probably wouldn't. And Sam would need him if the going got harder.

He glanced at Susan, decided she was safe there for the moment, and took a look in the next room. Jean lay on the bed, tied at the wrists and ankles, a gag over her mouth. She couldn't say anything, but her eyes spoke for her. They blazed with anger.

He laughed softly, imagining the way she could struggle. A conquest like that was worthwhile, and of much more value than what he had gotten from Susan.

She had practically thrown herself at him. Jean was of a different type. She would put up a battle.

"We'll be going home pretty soon," he told her. "Then we can get rid of these ropes. We'll get along, you and me."

He had walked up to the bed, and now, leaning over, he patted Jean's cheek. When she jerked away from his touch, he seemed amused.

"Won't be too long," he murmured. "You just lay there an' be patient."

He left her, locking the door, then glanced in at Susan, and wondered what to do with her. Then suddenly he knew. He had to do something about Glory, too. The two girls could be put in one package. Glory, who had been Alice Gould and who had good contacts, was a fool for money. It would cost a little, but if he put out the money, Glory would head for El Paso and take Susan with her. He started chuckling. What a perfect solution for Susan — to establish her in a goddamned parlor house. She was just right for it, and in a few months and after some sound experience, she might be pretty good.

Sam walked out on the porch. Kansas wasn't there but Al Durfree and several others were. He spoke to Al. "Find Glory, and see if Rupe Singer is somewhere around. Tell 'em I want to talk to 'em."

He scowled briefly. Rupe Singer might not fall in with such a plan, but it would be smart to include him. Of course, he really didn't have to worry. Glory would make the decision. As for Susan, she was no problem at all. Weepy and spineless, she would do as she was told.

CHAPTER
THIRTEEN

Linus wasn't quite sure what would happen when he got close to town, but nothing did. He reached the first houses, circled past them, and kept on riding, two streets away from the main street. Then, well into town, he swung in the direction of the business district. In the yard behind Sol Drews' he reined up, dismounted and tried the back door. It was locked, but after a little hammering, Sol opened the door, and gasped.

"Linus! Get in here, quick."

Linus stepped in. "What's all the excitement?"

"Wait till Holloway finds you're in town. You'll see plenty excitement. I figger —"

He broke off and raised his head. Linus had stiffened. Down the street, somewhere, they had heard a shot. Just a single shot — no more.

"Wonder what that was?" Sol said, and he was frowning. "It could be from the hotel."

"Holloway's there?"

"He's there and Weller Talbot just went in. He stopped here a minute, then he went on to the hotel. I couldn't stop him."

They were walking through the store as they talked, and now they looked through the front windows toward the hotel. Al Durfree, Dustin and Ellsworth were on the porch. Durfree was at the door, looking in, but from his attitude he didn't seem worried.

"Reckon I told Talbot the wrong thing," Sol muttered. "I said Susan had been with Sam Holloway earlier. They was at dinner at the hotel. Nothing wrong with that, but —"

"Have you seen Jean?"

Sol looked at him, then away. "Well, she might be with the Billings girls, or with someone else."

"Or she might be in the hotel — with Holloway. Sol, it makes me shaky just thinking about it."

Now Kansas was leaving the hotel. He slouched up the street to the Round Corral saloon, and went inside. Then something else attracted Linus' attention. Sam Holloway's so-called sister, Glory, and Rupe Singer were coming this way. He lost them for a moment, and when Rupe Singer came in sight again, he was alone. He angled for the Round Corral.

"Where do you think Glory went?" Linus asked.

"Probably stopped in to see Molly. Her dressmaking shop is just two doors from here."

"Maybe I ought to see her. Through her I might be able to get into the hotel."

"You'd better stay here where you're safe," the storekeeper advised. "We'll get Mac —"

"Sure, we'll get Mac," Linus said. "But in the meantime let me use your back door again."

Linus traveled from the back door of the store to Molly Carver's back door without being noticed. Molly's back door was locked, so he had to knock several times. She answered the knocking, looked startled when she recognized him, and started to close the door again.

Linus pushed it open and stepped inside. He grinned at her and said, "Molly, what's wrong? You used to like me."

She was a tall, thin spinster, and no longer young. An angular woman, stern and righteous, and a fountain of gossip. It was said she knew all the secrets in the valley — or could imagine them. It was probably true.

"Linus," she mumbled. "I —"

"Don't worry," Linus said. "I just want to see Glory."

He pushed toward the front of the store, entering Molly's cutting and fitting room, and there was Glory. She had taken off her dress, yet in several petticoats and a camisole, she was still almost enveloped with clothes.

With a pretty show of modesty, Glory reached for some dress material on the table. She draped part of it in front of her body and cried, "Why — why, Mr. Coleman! I just don't know what to say."

He smiled at her crookedly. "Don't you — Alice?"

The name was like a blow across the face. She stiffened, and her eyes narrowed. She spoke slowly, almost harshly. "My name is Glory Holloway."

"But in El Paso they called you Alice Gould."

She shook her head. "My name is Glory Holloway."

"That's not what Gail said."

"Who's Gail?"

"She works for Katie. And I understand Katie knows you, too."

"I'll have them run out of town — all of them."

She hadn't caved in. She remained defiant. But she had dropped the dress material, and her hands were clenched as she hit at him, her words high and excited. "You're not important any longer. You're already dead, Linus Coleman."

"Sure," Linus said. "But what about you?"

The woman looked toward Molly. "Ready me my dress."

Before Molly could answer, the bell attached to the front door which announced a customer's entrance started tingling. Linus glanced at the door separating them from the front room. He motioned to Molly, and spoke under his breath. "Why don't you see who it is? Maybe —"

That was as far as he got. Whoever had come in was at the door to the fitting room. As he pushed it open he called, "Hey, Glory. You still here somewhere? Sam wants you."

It was Al Durfree. And the first thing he must have seen when he opened the door was Glory in white petticoats and a camisole, putting on her dress. He gasped, rather normally, and started to back out. Then he saw Linus. He made a funny sound in his throat, and clawed at his holster gun.

Linus heard the blast of Durfree's gun as he was raising his own. He fired in answer, realizing Durfree had made the fatal mistake of hurrying his shot. He fired again as Durfree staggered backward, still trying to bring up his gun. Durfree stumbled and fell, striking a chair and breaking it on his way to the floor.

Molly had screamed while the shooting was going on, but she fainted promptly afterward. Linus heard her

176

slumping to the floor as he was still watching Durfree. Now he took a look at her — and at Glory, who had pulled her dress half on, then had seemed to freeze, unable to finish.

"Might be a good thing to get dressed," Linus said gruffly.

He knew that was a silly thing to say, but the words just popped into his head and he had spoken them. At any minute now, people might be charging inside to find out what the shooting had been about.

He moved to the front room, passing the motionless figure of Al Durfree. He walked to the window looking out on the main street. Through a lacy curtain he noticed several men down the street, staring this way. But one was running — Rupe Singer — and if his lame leg was hurting him, he ignored it. He had his gun drawn and he was nearly at the porch.

Linus raised the gun he was holding, but Singer was at an awkward angle, and Linus didn't shoot. Instead, he waited a few seconds until Singer reached the door, and plowed inside. The man shouted, "Glory, you all right? You —"

He broke off, saw Durfree on the floor, then caught sight of Linus by the window, and he swung that way, twisting his gun. But he didn't get to use it. Linus fired twice, driving one shot after the other. The first bullet started Singer backward. The second smashed him off balance. He staggered almost to the side wall before he fell.

Linus took another quick look through the window. The men on the street were still watching, but he couldn't see anyone hurrying this way. Probably the shots which had greeted Rupe Singer would discourage anyone else. But the front of this building would be watched, and in a few minutes the back door would be covered — maybe by Holloway's men. Anyhow, Linus didn't want to get trapped in here.

He swung away, charged through the cutting room, and no more than glanced at the two women. Molly hadn't come out of her faint, and Glory hadn't dressed. But when people came in, Glory would be in good shape to explain how he, Linus Coleman, had shot Al Durfree and then Rupe Singer — without even giving them a chance. She would hurt him all she could.

But he could worry about that later. He plowed out the back door, moving parallel to the main street and keeping behind buildings. Then, beyond the smithy, he turned toward the street. A few men were gathering in front of Molly Carver's, and as he watched, McMullen came in sight. He brushed past the others to enter the shop. Those nearby followed him.

With everyone staring that way, Linus risked crossing the street — and no one challenged him. He had marked two men in front of the Round Corral saloon, but neither was Kansas, and he wondered what had happened to him. He had gone into the saloon, must have been there when the shooting started. And then what — ?

Cutting back toward the rear of the saloon, he caught a glimpse of Kansas, and it surprised him to see the man playing cautious. Kansas hadn't impressed him as one who would duck out of sight if there was any danger around. More likely, he would cause it. But here the man was, back off the street where he might be safe. Then Linus smiled crookedly. He had been mistaken. Kansas wasn't back here to avoid trouble. He was on his way to Katie's.

Linus slowed down. He had started for the rear of the hotel, hoping he might get in that way — but what about Kansas? Of all of Holloway's men, Kansas seemed the most dangerous. And if the man could be isolated at Katie's, he, Linus, would have an easier time in the hotel. Katie, herself, might help him.

As he aimed at the passageway leading to Katie's he saw two men at the bank corner looking his way. He might have been seen crossing the street, too, or from several other points. But that couldn't be helped, and he hurried to Katie's door and knocked.

It was Katie herself who answered the door, and she didn't invite him in. Instead, she blocked his way, and she wasn't smiling. She seemed angry and her words were sharp. "My house isn't open. Come back tonight."

Linus shook his head. "He's in there, Katie."

"Who do you mean? I said we were closed."

"But Kansas just went inside."

"I tell you, no."

Linus raised one hand, pushed it against her well-corseted stomach, and said, "Back up, Katie. I'm coming in."

A voice behind her broke in. It was a man's voice and he seemed amused. "Let him in, Katie. Seems like he's askin' for it."

Linus took a deep breath. "Kansas?"

"Yep — waitin'."

Katie moved out of the way and as she stepped into some doorway, Linus could peer up the corridor. By night, he might not have been able to see a thing, or if the parlor door was open, the lamps on low, he might have seen a vague figure just ahead. That was what he could see now; a vague, indistinct figure. The fading daylight seeped past him and showed him that much. It didn't help a great deal.

"Come closer," Linus said.

The man laughed. "Why?"

"I want to be sure who I'm shooting."

"You ain't gonna shoot anyone," Kansas said. "If we was out in the sun an' you could see me, an' if you had a good start on me, you couldn't get off a single shot. I'm too damned fast."

"Then come on outside."

"Think I'm a fool?"

Linus was straining his eyes, trying to see the man more clearly. And his vision was improving. He could distinguish the man fairly well — not in detail, but as to size and position. And he could make out something else. Off to the side, tight against the wall, was another figure — a girl — one of the girls who lived here. What she was doing there and why she didn't flee he couldn't understand.

Then, in a way, Kansas explained her, for he said, "Gail honey, you just watch me. I want you to know what kind o' man you got. You ready, Coleman? Ain't we talked enough? I'm gonna count three, then cut you down."

180

Linus didn't speak. He watched the vague figure in the corridor. He had stiffened, his right hand close to his holster gun. What was going to happen in the next few seconds he didn't know. For years, he had known he was good with a gun, but he had never expected to have to test his ability against someone else. Then, suddenly, he had been pushed into a series of crises in which he had to depend on his gun. He had stayed alive — thus far. Against Kansas, however, and with the man half-hidden in shadows, what chance did he have?

Kansas was counting. The seconds were running out. "*One — Two — Three!*"

Linus whipped up his gun, falling sideways and firing as he did so. But strangely enough, no shots were fired back at him. Instead, down the corridor, Kansas was struggling with someone — the girl who had been flattened against the wall. It was Gail, for Kansas shouted her name as he fought with her.

"Damnit, Gail — look what you . . ."

The words trailed off, and as Linus moved along the corridor, Gail and Kansas dropped to the floor. A moment later, he reached them, stooped over, pushed the girl aside and took a look at Kansas. He was badly wounded, hit in the chest.

He spoke weakly and complainingly. "You never coulda got me in a fair fight. That damned girl. Shoulda broke her neck."

"He nearly did," Gail said.

She stood up, breathing heavily. Her dress was torn, her hair mussed up. There was a scratch across her face. Linus could see it even in this poor light.

"Without your help I might not have had a chance," Linus said.

She shook her head. "I didn't do it for you. I did it for myself. Don't ever be sorry about Kansas. He laughs and seems amusing, but with women he's a beast. If you want a reason to hate him, he's the one who killed Ken McMullen. He boasted of it last night."

"What else has he told you?"

The girl took a shaky breath. "I need a drink. I'm not supposed to take one this early, but Katie —" She raised her voice. "Hey, Katie."

Still on his knees, Linus found and picked up the gun Kansas had dropped. Then he stood up. Kansas hadn't spoken again. Probably he was unconscious, but he was still living.

Linus added his voice to Gail's, and called, "Hey, Katie. We want to see you."

She appeared in the corridor, and she didn't look happy. "This finishes everything," she moaned. "What can I do? Something like this never happened before in any of my houses."

"Forget it," Linus said. "Get a bottle of whiskey for Gail, and send someone for the doctor."

"She knows where my whiskey is," Katie said. "As for the doctor, I'll go myself. I feel sick."

She left by the side door. Gail had disappeared, too, probably on the way to get Katie's bottle. He stooped over Kansas, called his name, but he got no answer. Kansas was clinging to life, but without much strength. He might never wake up again.

Linus rolled a cigarette. The events of the late afternoon, at Molly Carver's and then here at Katie's, made him shaky inside, kept his nerves drawn to a high pitch. But his fingers behaved better than he expected. The cigarette he rolled looked very usual. He lit it and took a deep taste of the tobacco and thought of what lay still ahead.

He couldn't stay here, at Katie's. He couldn't wait for McMullen or go looking for him — expecting him to work out some miracle, and have a dozen fighting men at his back. He couldn't wait for the night, for the hotel would be lighted, and Holloway's men would be waiting. Jean, he was pretty sure, was a prisoner in the hotel. He was afraid Susan was there, too. Most likely, Sam wouldn't have hurt them — or at least he hoped he was right about that.

Linus took another taste of the tobacco, then called for Gail. She didn't answer, and after a moment he decided she wouldn't. She probably was blaming herself for what had happened to Kansas. It might take a lot of whiskey to drown her memories.

He walked back to the side door and looked out toward the rear of the hotel. The Talbot wagon was there, but he knew the bed of the wagon was empty. On this side of it ran a low fence and beyond the wagon stood a cottonwood. From several of its branches clotheslines were strung to the rear of the hotel. On a bench sat two tubs. This arrangement was for men stopping at the hotel who wanted to do some washing. The lines weren't in use right now. Maybe at the moment, as happened occasionally, the hotel had no other guests except Holloway and his crowd.

Linus could see no one in sight. He checked his gun, re-loaded it, then slid it back in its holster, stepped outside and started for the hotel.

CHAPTER
FOURTEEN

Sam Holloway paced the lobby of the hotel, smoking the stubby end of a cigar, now and then spitting out chunks of profanity. Actually, he was thinking, hard and imaginatively. He kept grimly at it, weighing one possibility against another, measuring every contingent he could think of. He was hard-headed enough to realize he had been driven into a corner. But he didn't mean to stay there. He meant to get out. If he used his head — and if he used the people he controlled — if he lied well and had a little luck, he still would ride through this bit of trouble he had blundered into. At least he would get away.

A few minutes ago there had been some shooting up the street, and Les Harper had investigated. The story he brought back seemed incredible — both Al Durfree and Rupe Singer were dead, and at the hands of Linus Coleman. But it was foolish to be amazed. If he got the drop on them, of course he could have killed them. And that must have been what happened.

But if Al and Rupe were dead, at least Kansas was still around, and Turk Kiley should be riding in almost any time now. What had happened to Turk Kiley he

185

didn't know. But damn it, Turk Kiley wasn't the kind to run out. He could count on him — if he ever got here.

In the meantime, along with himself and Kansas, he had Les Harper, Fred Dustin, Sim Ellsworth and Jim Rawls. Good men, used to handling their guns. Maybe they didn't rate with Kansas but at least they were dependable. If they only —

He broke off his thinking, raised his head and listened. A single shot had broken the stillness. He waited for another, for several more — but that was all: a single shot. The explosion seemed close to the hotel, but from the rear, or maybe from a nearby building.

"Now what the hell was that?" Dustin asked.

"Bullet shot," Sam grunted. "Out back. Might mean something. Might not."

"Wish we was outa this," Dustin muttered.

"We'll ride out soon as it's dark. We'll take the wagon out back. Take the wrapped-up body, Talbot's body, and the two girls."

"I don't like takin' the girls."

"Where did you get so damned holy?"

"It ain't that," Dustin said. "It's just that — well, a town can get sore as hell if any of the womenfolks have been hurt. I mean, if it was just us —"

"Cut it out," Sam broke in, motioning angrily with both arms. "We are caught in this fix, and there's only two ways to go. We can bluff it out or we can give up. Give up and we get a rope around the neck. That what you want?"

"No one said anything about givin' up," Dustin snapped. "I'll just be glad when this is over."

"Me, too," Ellsworth said.

"You earn damn good money," Sam said. "You want it for nothing?"

He glared at them. They were good men. They had been loyal, dependable, but now and then he had to slap them down. He opened his mouth to start nagging, but changed his mind. The hell with it. He would tear into them some other time.

Jim Rawls, watching from the lobby window, asked a question which was beginning to worry Sam himself. "Can't figger what happened to Kansas. Just went after a bottle. Shoulda been back before this."

"He'll get back," Sam said.

He walked to the window himself, stared out into the street. Here and there were a few people, and along the tie rails a few horses and two teams and wagons. Nothing unusual in the scene. He could almost wonder why he was staying here in the hotel.

Standing there, scowling, he took another careful look at the situation, and he tried to look at it honestly. Without much question, Coleman and the sheriff knew a good deal about him. At least they had dug up Coleman's father. They probably had shown this evidence to Weller Talbot and his daughters, but Talbot was dead and the two girls were here where they couldn't talk. Of course, Coleman and the sheriff could have talked to a number of other people, but talk wasn't evidence.

At the present moment, if a crowd broke in, and could get to the girls, and the two bodies, he might have to do some tall explaining, but things weren't going to go that far. He thought he knew just what Coleman and McMullen were facing. If a man knew the facts, he could get somewhere, but working on rumors, men hung back. Who wanted to risk getting hurt in a battle where the issue wasn't clear?

"We ain't supposed to be pinned down here," Sam said, thinking aloud. "But it still might be a good idea to keep someone watching the back door. How about you, Harper?"

The man shrugged. "Sure. I'll take the back door."

He turned that way, heading down the corridor. Sam watched him out of sight, then looked up the street again. He nearly smiled. Hell — what was he worried about? The street out there was calm as a Sunday, and in about an hour it would grow dark. Then they would get a team and —

His thoughts were interrupted by crashing gunfire, and it seemed so near that as he whirled around, he thought the fight was right here in the lobby. Then he realized the explosions came from down the corridor, where he had sent Harper. He started that way, but stopped — and just in time. Fred Dustin, ahead of him, reached the corridor but was met by a blast of gunfire. It hurled him backward and sideways and he hit the floor and didn't get up again.

Even in this moment of confusion Sam could guess what had happened. Harper, who had been sent to the rear door, hadn't gotten there soon enough, or maybe hadn't done his job. At any rate, someone had moved into the hotel, and right now the man had control of

the corridor. Sam could even guess the man's name —
Linus Coleman.

He stepped to the wall near the head of the corridor,
glanced at Ellsworth and Jim Rawls, and then shouted,
"Coleman! Linus Coleman!"

The man down the corridor didn't answer. Sam
shouted at him, but still got no answer. He muttered
profanely under his breath, looked at Ellsworth and Jim
Rawls and suddenly wondered what he was going to do
next.

In some way or other, he had to get Coleman out of
the corridor, and that might not be easy. It struck
across his mind that the way things were working out,
he might have to bust from the hotel and run to save
his hide. But he didn't want to do that. If only Kansas
would show up. Where was he, anyhow? Could it be
possible that Kansas had walked out?

He shook his head and started thinking, hard. He
didn't notice that both Jim Rawls and Sim Ellsworth
had edged toward the front door.

There were six rooms on each side of the corridor.
Linus Coleman stood in the entrance to one of those at
the rear. He had had no trouble reaching the hotel, but
as he had started in he had run into a man walking
toward him. The man had grabbed his gun, but not
quickly enough. Then another man had shown up, at
the head of the corridor. He had had his gun in his
hand and had been lifting it when Linus fired.

"Coleman," someone in the lobby shouted. "Linus
Coleman!"

He didn't bother to answer, but reloaded his gun, and stood waiting. The man in the lobby shouted his name again, and probably that man was Sam Holloway. He hoped so.

The room behind him was empty, except for the usual furniture. Linus looked up the corridor toward the lobby, could see no one, and took the chance to cross the corridor to the opposite door. This room wasn't empty. On the floor was the blanket-wrapped body of his father, and on the bed was another body — Weller Talbot's. His face was the color of putty, the mouth sagging open, the eyes wide-open but sightless. Only a little blood showed on his shirt front. Very probably, he had bled mostly from the back.

Linus took a look at Talbot on the bed, another at the blanketed figure on the floor, then from the room's doorway he stared bleakly toward the lobby. Here, just behind him, was the justification for his being here. But there was more justification: the De Sellums, Ken, McMullen, even Erb Wylie. And maybe Susan and Jean. Abruptly remembering the girls he wondered where they were, and as he thought of Weller Talbot and what had happened to him, his muscles tightened. Ahead of him were other rooms. He could work forward, try the next two — but he was almost afraid to look, afraid of what he might find.

"Holloway!" he shouted. "I want to see you."

The man laughed, and from the sound he didn't seem at all worried. "So you want to see me, huh? Walk straight ahead."

Linus fingered his gun. It occurred to him that in all probability Holloway could leave by the front door any time he wished. All he had to do was walk out, cross to his horse and ride. Of course if he did he would be leaving some things at the hotel which would need explanation — undoubtedly if he left now he wouldn't be able to come back. So maybe — for a time — he wouldn't pull out. Maybe he still thought he could win out.

"How many men you got in the lobby?" he called.

"Plenty," Holloway answered. "Come an' count 'em."

Linus shook his head. Two were too many, if they were on opposite sides of the corridor. To walk out there, or to dive out and take his chances, was crazy even to think about.

Holloway spoke suddenly. "Jim, where the hell do you think you're going?"

"Thought I might slip around to the back door," a voice answered. "Then we can box this fellow Coleman."

"You're sure that's where you're goin'?"

"Where else, Sam?"

"By God, if you try to run out —"

Now that Linus could understand the talk in the lobby, he ventured a caustic comment. "Better get out while you can, mister. And any of the rest of you, too. Pull out before it's too late. Before —"

But that time had already come. A voice shouted from outside — McMullen's voice. It rang with authority. "Holloway, we want to talk to you. Come out on the porch."

Holloway didn't yell any answer. Maybe he was too startled. Surely, he must have been surprised at any challenge from the street.

"I said, come out on the porch," McMullen shouted again. "Come on out or we'll be in after you."

Holloway still didn't reply. Maybe he was peering into the street — something Linus would have liked to do. For this new development was damned interesting. Right here in town, and rather quickly, McMullen must have rounded up a crowd. Or maybe he was bluffing. Maybe he was almost alone.

"What we gonna do?" a voice in the lobby asked. "We could hit for the back door wasn't for Coleman."

"He's only one man, anyhow," another voice said. "We wouldn't have a chance in the street."

Linus was glad now that he was back toward the rear of the corridor. He raised his voice a little. "Sure, come this way. Who wants to be first? I sure will get the man who's first."

He grinned sourly. He could appreciate the problem these men had. Almost certainly, the first man to try the corridor would go down. And he might get the second before those behind them could spot exactly where he was, and aim their guns. Yes, it was going to be a tough problem to determine who would be the first to hit the corridor.

He spoke again. "Come ahead. I'm waiting. Holloway, why don't you be first?"

"By God, maybe I will," the man answered, and his words were sharp, terse.

192

"Here's your last chance," McMullen shouted from the street. "This goes for your men, too, Holloway. Walk out, peaceful like, or we'll be in after you."

Listening in the corridor, Linus heard the man mutter something. He had made a decision, and he must have whispered it to his men, for suddenly, and with no warning at all, he appeared at the head of the hallway. He broke silence, then, shouting, "All right, Coleman. Here I am. If you —"

Even as he spoke, he dived for the floor, and whipped three shots from his gun, fanning the narrow space between the two rows of rooms. He screamed, "Elly — Jim — get him!" And he twisted his head to look back.

Probably, Holloway had led the charge into the corridor, and had planned to dive to the floor, leaving the men behind him to catch the shots Linus would fire. But things hadn't worked out that way. No one followed him. As he looked back and saw no one, then looked ahead, a shocked expression came over his face. For even as he saw Linus and tried to aim his gun that way, he must have noticed the other's gun blasting straight at him.

As Linus squeezed the trigger, Holloway jerked. He got nearly to his knees, then collapsed and fell on his face. He didn't move again.

Suddenly Linus heard McMullen's voice from the lobby, ordering someone to throw down his guns, then telling someone else to collect them and to see to it that the arrested men were taken to the jail. In the next breath he shouted, "Hey, Linus, you all right?"

"Seem to be," Linus answered.

He started forward but before he was halfway to the lobby the door to one of the front rooms opened and Susan appeared. She looked at Sam Holloway's figure almost at her feet, and she caught her breath; then she glanced down the corridor, saw Linus and stumbled toward him. Her clothing was torn, her hair was mussed and her eyes were swollen from crying. As she reached Linus she threw herself in his arms. If he hadn't held her she would have fallen.

McMullen entered the corridor, looked down at Holloway's body, touched it with the toe of his boot, then noticed Linus and Susan. He asked, "How is she?"

"Think she's going to be all right," Linus said as McMullen walked toward them. Then he added, "Here, hold her."

He practically shoved Susan into the sheriff's arms, and turned away.

"Hey, what's the idea?" McMullen cried. "Where you going?"

"Want to see if Jean's here," Linus answered.

He found her in the other front room, bound and gagged on the bed. His heart gave a jump as he saw her. He cried her name, and a moment later, when he realized she didn't seem to be hurt he felt suddenly weak. His hands were clumsy as he untied her. Then he helped her stand up, his arms around her.

He thought, *This is wrong. I should be holding Susan.* Then he shook his head and realized it was Jean he had been worried about, it was Jean who was important. He wasn't exactly sure when this had

194

happened in his thinking, but he knew now it was so. His arms tightened.

"I can stand up alone," Jean said.

He looked down at her. "Do you mind this?"

"Not at all," she said instantly. "Just — keep it up."

"That's what I'm planning," Linus said.

McMullen took charge of the clean-up work. A posse was sent to the Coleman ranch to pick up the men who were there. In the morning another delegation went to view the graves in the north grove.

McMullen questioned the two arrested men, Jim Rawles and Sim Ellsworth. He talked to Katie and the girls who worked for her. All at once there was more evidence than was needed for the court hearing that would follow. Holloway hadn't bought the Coleman ranch. He and his men had simply taken it, and they had frightened away the De Sellums. Linus would be able to return to his home.

"I suppose that means you'll be getting married," McMullen said. "Susan?"

"No," Linus said. "Jean."

"Didn't know you had that much sense. What'll happen to Susan?"

Linus shrugged. "Who knows? She's pretty as ever. Someone will grab her. Maybe she's learned something from Holloway."

"No. People don't learn that quickly. Wouldn't want to guess what'll happen to her. How did you get away from her?"

"She got mad when I turned her over to you, to look for Jean. She stayed mad. Then I've got a sneaky notion Jean told her what was what."

McMullen smiled. "Trust a woman to handle a woman. By the way, there's a new girl at Katie's. She goes by the name of Alice Gould. Used to be called Glory."

Linus looked away. "I told her she'd end up there, but I didn't mean —"

"People climb or they sink to their own level — the place they fit. What else would you have expected?"

It was growing dusk. Jean, Susan and their mother were staying temporarily with the Findleys in town, and tonight, very soon, he would go there. He knew Susan wouldn't be present. She would stay in her room or go out. But Jean and her mother would make the evening pleasant.

McMullen was in for a harder time. He and his wife would miss Ken for a long time. The kind of loss they had suffered left scars which had to be carried. They couldn't be forgotten easily.

But McMullen tried. He looked up at the sky and smiled. "It's going to be a good night — and a good day tomorrow."

"Sure," Linus nodded. "A good night and if we work at it, good days ahead."